BONDS OF THE GODDESS

GRECIAN GODDESS TRILOGY: BOOK 3

TESSA COLE

CLARA WILS

Gryphon's Gate Publishing

Bonds of the Goddess

Copyright © 2021 Tessa Cole & Clara Wils

Cover Design by CReya-tive

Gryphon's Gate Publishing

550 King St. N.

PO Box 42088 Conestoga

Waterloo, ON

N2L 6K5

ebook ISBN: 978-1-988115-94-8

Print ISBN: 978-1-988115-93-1

Bonds of the Goddess

by Tessa Cole and Clara Wils

CHAPTER 1

ANNIE

I FELL, THE WORLD SPINNING: SKY, BUILDINGS, GROUND, SKY, buildings, ground, over and over, around and around.

My initial scream at having been flung out the window of Hera's high rise died as the aching emptiness of losing my bonds with my guys filled me and the certainty that this was it. I didn't have Del's powers anymore, I couldn't make myself float, and Rion was unconscious and couldn't fly out to save me.

Sky, buildings, Janice—

Janice!

She'd been caught up in Hera's gust as well, and just like me was spinning, her screams having died off too. What was the point? We were dead and there wasn't anything we could do about it.

She spun out of sight, then back into sight, then out, then—

Was way too close, swooping toward me with—

Holy-what-the-fuck!

Were those wings?

She seized my arm just before I hit the ground, and wrenched me up, making my stomach lurch at the sudden change of direction.

My heart pounded so hard it shook me with every throbbing beat, and my thoughts whirled.

I was just—

I jerked my gaze up to the top of the high rise where I'd fallen.

I was dead. I was sure I was going to die, then—

My attention jumped to Janice.

Then—

Then—

It was as if I couldn't comprehend that Janice had wings. She wasn't like me... was she?

She set me down, but between my shattered and sliced calves—from going over the balcony railing—and my own jelly-legs from thinking I was about to die, I simply sagged in a heap on the sidewalk.

Janice sat heavily next to me. One of her wings curled around before her and she stared at it, looking as stunned as I felt. Her feathers were large and long and a gorgeous golden-brown like hawk wings and not like Rion's white angel wings. Then her attention jerked to me.

"Did you do this?" she demanded.

Me?

"You're a goddess," she said. "Did you give me wings?"

Had I?

No. I couldn't have. Even if I'd been able to think past falling to my death, I couldn't give someone wings. I couldn't even give someone powers... could I?

No. I hadn't given the guys their powers. They gained

their powers by entering my world, and when I bonded with them, I got their powers as well. And I was pretty sure I hadn't bonded with Janice.

My chest squeezed, my soul searching for the bonds with my guys that were no longer there.

I'd lost them—

But they were still alive and with Hera right this very minute. I had to save them, had to—

"Annie, did you give me wings?" Janice pressed, yanking my attention back to her.

"No," I said, but my voice was so shaky, I wasn't sure it had come out clear. "No," I repeated, trying to be firm, but too much was going on and I couldn't stop trembling.

"Then what the hell is this?" she asked, her voice also shaky.

She crossed her arms over her now bare breasts, covering herself in a weak attempt at modesty and an even weaker attempt to stay warm against the freezing temperature. It seemed an unfortunate side effect of the wings having sprout out her back was that they'd ripped off everything she'd been wearing above the waist.

People were gawking at us and a crowd was gathering nearby. Of course I couldn't blame them. Even if they hadn't seen us fall, Janice was topless and had wings.

Murmurs rippled around us.

"It's an angel!"

"That was some stunt. I don't even see the safety chute."

"I wonder what they're promoting?"

"We should get out of here," I forced out, my attention

jumping back to the top of the building where my guys were as I tried to stagger to my feet.

Agony screamed through my body, reminding me I needed to heal myself, and that even if I could fix myself with what little magic I had left, I'd still be helpless against Hera.

Hell, me with all of my guys' powers and all of my guys, along with Janice and her gun hadn't been enough to bring down Hera.

I channeled my healing power to my legs, strengthening them as I mended the broken bones and pushed out the glass shards. My back was cold and in pain. I'd gone through a window backward. My shirt was still mostly on, enough that I didn't care about the cold, but I healed the wounds there as well.

Standing—successfully this time—I helped Janice up as well.

Now that I was on my feet, I could see large men in tactical gear with automatic rifles, running toward us from Hera's building.

Well, fuck.

"We need to get out of here. Now," I said, my voice stronger this time. Looking around, I quickly got my bearings. We were across the street from Macy's downtown.

My mind spun into action as I recalled an article I'd read about the pedway, a series of tunnels creating a whole underground city below downtown. I'd never gone down there myself, but there supposed to be an entrance from Macy's.

I grabbed Janice's arm and hustled her across the

street, not caring about traffic. Luckily, we weren't hit, though there was a lot of honking and curses thrown our way.

Once inside Macy's, I instantly felt better. Who didn't feel better inside Macy's? The trouble was, Janice's feathery wings had barely gotten through the door and would be an issue now that we were inside.

"Can you get rid of those things?" I asked.

"I don't even know where they came from!"

"Well try," I snapped back.

That seemed to jolt some sense into her and she blinked as her gaze swept around the store as if she'd just realized where we were.

"Right, sorry." She frowned, then squeezed her eyes shut, then scrunched up her face, and for a second I was afraid she wouldn't be able to do it.

Then her wings vanished. One second they were there, the next they weren't, they didn't even melt away like Rion's did. Just poof.

She snagged a shirt from a nearby rack and pulled it on and we hurried deeper into the store.

"Hey!" a woman with the look of a store employee called out, racing toward us. "You can't just..."

"FBI!" Janice shouted a little too forcefully, her shock still evident as she held up her badge on the lanyard still around her neck.

The clerk stumbled to a stop, her expression shocked.

And because we didn't have time to waste, I took advantage of that shock. "Where's your entrance to the pedway? The underground thingy?" I asked, as assertively as possible.

"Over there." The clerk pointed toward a bank of escalators heading to the basement.

Right, of course. That should have been obvious, but I was running on pure adrenaline and was barely thinking. In fact, I was stunned I was thinking at all... which was just par for the course the last couple of weeks.

We ran from the still baffled clerk and hit the escalators as men stormed into the store behind us, and I prayed they'd have no clue about the pedway's layout, because I certainly didn't. My hope was to lose them and hide somewhere without getting lost myself. At least Janice was running on her own now, and I wasn't having to drag her along.

Everything became a blur. We ran from hall to hall, trying to avoid larger open areas. Finally, we came to the door of a service area. A janitor had just come out and was walking away, and I managed to stick my foot in the door before it closed and locked itself.

We slid in, pulling the door closed and leaned against the cinderblock walls trying to gasp for air as quietly as possible.

I was fairly certain we'd lost Hera's men, but I didn't want to risk it, and the second we had a little bit of breath back, we continued running.

I didn't know how long later it was when we finally rushed, out of breath, through a metal security door into a dimly lit, short hall. We sagged onto the floor, leaning against the wall behind the door so if it opened, we'd be hidden behind it, gasping and trembling.

"Holy fuck," Janice said, once she'd managed to catch her breath again. "Did that just happen?"

"Yep," I said, unable to stop myself from shaking. "But I couldn't explain it to you." All I really knew was that Hera had handed our asses to us and she still had my guys.

My chest squeezed again and I fought to breathe past the emptiness inside me.

"So ah..." Janice frowned, turned her back to me, and pulled up her newly acquired shirt, showing me her back. "Are there... markings or something? Am I bleeding?"

Her back was smooth and clear with no indication she'd ever grown wings.

"There's nothing."

She pulled her shirt down. "So just bam, I have wings? Then I don't? What sort of fucked up world is this?"

Except I had a sneaking suspicion that it wasn't *this* world that was the reason.

"I think... well, those guys I was with..." How did I put this without sounding crazy? Except Janice already knew about my magic and Hera, so hey, another world was just another detail.

"The guys are from another world where people have wings and can put them away when they're done. It's crazy, but it's true. I've seen it. I'm guessing you have some of that in your blood, probably from an ancient ancestor. It must have come out when you needed it most, I guess... maybe?"

"That's insane," she scoffed then frowned. "And yet... I have wings... so... what the fuck?" She snarled the last word, a mix of emotions rushing across her expression. She was upset and shocked and confused. I could understand that. Her world had just been turned upside down. I'd been there not that long ago.

"Someday I'll take you to this place and you can see for yourself. For now, we just need to survive." And I needed to get my guys back.

The pain in my chest clenched tight again, stealing my breath and a new realization hit me. Our bonds were gone and they'd watched me be thrown out a window. They probably thought I was dead.

For all I knew, *they* were dead.

I didn't know how everything had gone so wrong, and I could only hope Hera, being the sick fuck that she was, would want to savor my guys' suffering and keep them alive long enough for me to figure out how to save them.

Gods, please.

Except what else could I do? She was so damned powerful.

And yet, I couldn't just give up.

She had my guys!

"This is so messed up." *I* was messed up. I was stupid enough to think we stood a chance against a three-thousand-year-old goddess.

"At least you didn't sprout wings," Janice said, her voice thick with exhaustion and frustration as she tried to crane her neck and see her back.

No, but my bonds with the guys had been severed. I was so very alone and scared and I didn't know what to do. I should have never even considered going up against Hera. I wasn't a hero. Sure, I'd been given some powers, but... I didn't know how to fight crime. I was a quiet administrative professional. That's what I was good at.

Not... trying to take down supervillains! What had I been thinking?

"We should probably go... somewhere," I said, my voice weak and uncertain. "Any ideas where?"

"Ah..." Janice still seemed distracted, as if she was stuck on the fact that she had wings. Which I could totally understand. "What? Sorry?"

"Where should we go? I can't go home and you shouldn't either. I'm guessing you can't go back to work. Hera will probably know if we go anywhere we'd usually go. We could try to get a hotel room somewhere, but I don't have a lot of cash on me and she can probably track credit cards and things. We need to stay off grid." But that left us with little to no options.

"I... uh... I think I might know a place." Janice dragged her gaze from staring off into space and back to me, but her eyes were still filled with shock. She hadn't fully come to grips with everything that had happened to us yet.

I wasn't sure I had either.

"There's this drug house," she said. "We took down some cartel guys there a couple weeks ago. It's empty now, and I can get us there if you have cab fare."

"Yeah, I think I have enough for that. Where is it?"

"Out in Oakbrook."

I raised my brows. "Swanky."

That was a nice neighborhood. My dad had doctor friends who lived out there, high-end surgeons who made a killing doing brain-stuff and heart-things.

I wasn't sure I had enough cash to get us there by taxi, but I could probably get us most of the way.

"Now we just need to get out of here and back to street level." I stood and looked around. There was the door we'd come through, next to where we'd collapsed, another at the end of the short hallway that said ELEC-TRICAL on it, and a third that said STORAGE. Our only way out was to go back into the hall we'd just come from.

And just as I thought that, the door started to open.

Crap. Hera's men had found us.

CHAPTER 2

ANNIE

PANIC SEIZED ME. THE ONLY SMALL CHANCE WE HAD TO escape was to fight and the best way to do that was to strike before they expected it, make an opening, and run like hell.

I jerked in front of the opening door and punched before I could lose my nerve. My fist slammed against a face dusted with stubble, but I no longer had Keph's strength and the impact jarred up my arm, probably hurting me more than the guy I'd just struck.

The man grunted and stumbled, his shoulder hitting the doorframe, and brilliant blue-green eyes widened with shock, capturing me.

My pulse lurched. "Del?"

He's alive. He's here. Thank God.

"Yeah," he said, rubbing his jaw. "You hit me."

I threw my arms around him and he easily plucked me up, lifting me from the ground in a tight embrace.

"Thank the gods you're alive and safe!" I said, though

I didn't know if he heard it with my face buried in his chest.

"I'm the only one," he said, his voice grim as he set me on my feet but kept his arms tight around me.

The only one? Were the others dead? Had I killed them by insisting on confronting Hera?

"How did you find us?" Janice asked.

"I threw myself out the window after you, but my ability to manipulate the water within me is more like floating than flying. It took me a moment to reach the ground and when I did, I noticed you running into that building. At first, I didn't know where you'd gone, but then..." He hooked a finger under my chin and urged me to look up at him. Pain filled his stunning eyes, the same aching heartache I felt. "I can't feel you anymore... The bond...?"

I tried to swallow around the lump in my throat. "It's gone. Hera took it somehow."

"Gods," he breathed, the muscles in his jaw tightening. "I could *feel* your water. So I followed that and found you here."

"Feel her water?" Janice asked.

"It's his magic," I said, not looking away from Del. "What about the others?"

"Hera has them. I saw them all caught up in bubbles of wind, unable to move," he replied. "I was the only one who escaped."

But they were still alive.

Thank God. Thank any and all gods.

Except how long would Hera keep them alive? Would she drain them of their powers as she had her previous harem? Would she torment them? Or would she get bored and just kill them.

"We have to rescue them." But I was exhausted, Janice was rattled, and Hera would likely be on guard, expecting a rescue attempt. Even if we were at full power and unexpected, we still didn't stand a chance, not without one hell of a good plan. "Fuck!"

"We need to rest. We need help. We need…" Del ran a hand through his long, blue-black hair, pushing it out of his face. "Gods, I don't know. She was so much more powerful than I expected."

"We can go to my safe house for now," Janice said.

"Safe house?" Del frowned. "What's that?"

"Exactly what it sounds like," Janice said, rolling her eyes at him as if he was an idiot for not knowing— because she probably hadn't fully registered on the fact that he was from a different world. "A *safe* house."

He nodded with a grimace. Then, he looked at her, cocking his head in curiosity. "I saw you sprout wings, *aurai* wings."

"Or-eye?" Janice sounded out the word.

"Are they different from Rion?" I asked as Del glanced back into the hall we'd come from then motioned that it was clear.

"Yes. Rion is *erinai*. *Aurai* are nymphs of the high mountains," Del replied, confidently heading down the hall as if he knew where he was going. "Some spend all their time in the skies, rarely landing. Their wings are different, more like an eagle's. Whereas Rion's are more like a falcon's, built for speed and lower-level flight."

A falcon's wings were different from an eagle's? I had

no clue... and really, I didn't want to get into it now. It wasn't really important.

"So I'm a nymph?" Janice said with a harrumphing laugh. "Some of my boyfriends would beg to differ."

"I don't know what you are," Del said. "You're of this world, so you shouldn't have wings at all... or so I thought. Although..." His frown deepened. "I suppose if my people came and went from this world in ages past, then perhaps some seed of my kind could still remain here. Very odd though."

"Lucky," I said with a shiver. If she hadn't sprouted wings, we'd both be dead.

"Very," Janice said in a similar tone, likely coming to the same realization.

Del led us to a wide set of stairs with a cold wind blowing down them and we climbed up onto a busy, snowy street where Janice flagged down a cab. We took it to Oakbrook, and I paid with the last of my cash, since I couldn't risk using my credit cards or going to a bank or ATM to withdraw more.

Luckily Janice's safe house was a fully furnished mansion set back on a large piece of property and there was even some food still in the fridge and pantry.

We picked through what wasn't expired or moldy, eating a meal in solemn silence around a table in the breakfast nook of an enormous luxury kitchen. I tried not to look like I was panicking, but my heart and thoughts had never stopped racing, even if the rest of me was starting to slow from exhaustion.

I had to rescue the others.

But I couldn't, not without an army. And even then, how would we do it?

Gods, I had no idea.

I only knew that I had to rescue them...

I had to—

Those thoughts just kept circling around and around in my mind, making me more frustrated and sad.

The food tasted like dust, but I didn't know if that was because it had come from boxes and had been sitting around, or because my soul hurt from the emptiness inside me.

Janice found a stash of liquor and we all had a tall glass to try to calm ourselves.

It didn't work. Now I was tipsy and panicking.

"Janice," Del said softly.

The woman turned to him. She still didn't look well. The realization that she was something other than human still pinched her expression. "Yes?"

"Might I have a moment alone with Annie?"

She looked from him to me a few times then topped up her glass with the amber liquid from the whiskey bottle and headed out of the kitchen, stopping at the large archway and half turning back to us. "It's a large house. I'll be... somewhere else... for as long as you need."

I didn't understand what she meant by that until she was gone and Del was suddenly very close, wrapping his arms around me in a comforting embrace.

"I'm sorry for all of this Annie," he said softly.

I melted into him, burying my face in his chest and sobbed, unable to hold my tears back. I was so lost and shaken. My body hurt, my soul hurt, and I couldn't hold it in and look strong anymore, especially with his arms around me.

He held me tight for a long moment then pressed his lips against the top of my head and murmured, "This is all my fault. Our fault. Us guys. We asked too much of you. You gave us so much and we just kept asking for more. We pushed you and ourselves beyond our limits and now..." His voice choked up and I thought I heard a faint sniffle.

I looked up at him then through the river flowing from my eyes, and he smiled softly. There was indeed a tear in his eye, just the one, but the hurt in his expression spoke of something deeper than just that single tear.

"Is it the same for you?" he asked, his voice heart-breakingly soft. "Like a limb has been cut off?"

I nodded.

"Only I imagine it must be worse for you. You lost all four of us and we only lost you."

I nodded again, unable to speak. The pain and the emptiness consumed me, threatening to drag me into darkness.

But then... I had Del. He was right here, and one kiss could fix everything.

Urgency flooded me, and I tangled my fingers in his hair, drawing him down to kiss me.

He caught on quickly, lifting me and meeting my lips halfway, and I kissed him with all the hunger born from the void inside me. He matched my intensity, our kiss turning ferocious in our desperate desire to rekindle the bond between us that wasn't reforming.

My grip tightened in his hair and his embrace turned to steel. It had taken just one kiss on the lips before, but no matter how long or hard we mashed our mouths together, the bond didn't return.

No light. No warmth. Nothing.

Finally, with my heart breaking, Del released me and sagged back onto a chair. My soul and body throbbed with emptiness and unfulfilled desire, and I followed him, straddling him to stay close, unable to deal with the physical separation in the face of our spiritual one.

I needed him. Needed him in me, his soul, his body, anything, something, please. Even if it was just for a moment, even if it wasn't our permanent bond. I couldn't be without him. Not right now.

"Perhaps we need to do more than kiss this time," he said, a mix of hope and desolation in his sea-green eyes as he wrapped his arms around me, steadying me in his lap.

"Yes. Of course," I replied, realization snapping through me. I jerked to my feet and yanked off my shirt even as a part of me trembled with the fear that sex wouldn't be enough.

But it had to be. I didn't know how I'd live with the ache inside me.

I shoved my pants off as Del stood and started to strip as well.

He quickly unbuttoned his shirt and shrugged out of it, revealing his gorgeous, sculpted chest, arms, and abs, then stepped out of his slacks, his erection springing free, large and proud.

The first time I'd seen him, he'd been sitting on that

rock, naked and erect, and I'd thought I'd been in a dream.

In a way it had been... and still was. His ridiculously wonderful cock was now mine. *He* was mine and I was his, and I was going to do whatever it took to claim him once again, to turn this nightmare back into the wonderful dream it had originally been.

We crashed back together, our lips hungry and desperate, and he sat back on the chair, drawing me down to straddle his lap as I wrapped my fingers around his cock. Not that he needed any working up. I was the one who needed help getting wet enough to take him inside me, but I had to have my hands on him, caressing him, feeling him, being connected with him in any small way that I could.

I stroked my hand from his base to his tip, squeezing hard, perhaps too hard, though at least I didn't have Keph's strength this time, and savored his shuddering groan into my mouth.

"Let me know when you want me," he said, his voice gruff with desire, his fingers roughly tormenting me, teasing through my folds and building up my own slick need.

"You'll come on command?" I gasped as he ground his thumb against my clit, the sensation just on the wrong side of painful.

But I didn't care. I was angry and empty and pain was something. Pain was what I needed, a way to release the furious heartache threatening to consume me.

"I'll come when you say."

He shoved two fingers inside me, his thumb still hard

against my clit, and my body trembled at the invasion. I dug my nails into his shoulder as my grip on his erection tightened and rocked my hips against his hand, but it wasn't enough. I needed him inside me.

"Fuck me," I hissed. *Fuck me until I can't think straight, until I can't feel, until I've forgotten how terrified I am. Fuck me until our souls bond again. Please.*

I leaned back and aligned him with my opening. He pulled his fingers out, and I impaled myself on him in one hard stroke. He was too much, too large. I wasn't completely ready for him and I didn't care. I took him all the way to the hilt, crying out with pain and heartache, trembling with a small, pathetic orgasm.

My breath hitched with disappointment then Del rubbed his thumb over my clit, making my orgasm blossom into a soft full-body shudder. My release, still too small, swept through me, and for a flickering second I forgot my pain. We were connected, even if it was only in body, and I could lose myself in him... over and over again until I was too exhausted to cry.

Still trembling, I pressed a finger to his lips. "Remember, you don't come until I say so."

He nodded stiffly.

"Good."

Then I began to lose myself in the bliss of his amazing body, rocking myself to even greater heights, tears leaking from my eyes.

CHAPTER 3

DELPHON

By all the gods, I wasn't sure I'd be able to keep my promise. Annie was, by far, the most incredible and sexy woman I'd ever known, and she was lost in lust and heartache—the same heartache that threatened to consume me. Her eyes were semi-glazed as she took her pleasure from me, over and over again, working herself, hard and needful, until she stiffened and shuddered with yet another orgasm. Then she began again. Her nails dug into my skin, her head thrown back with the desperate, feral cries of a hunger she couldn't sate, a black pit inside her that she couldn't fill.

And through all this, I felt like I would explode within her. Yet somehow, by some miracle, I held myself back, tense and rigid. I was at the peak of my own bliss, but couldn't enjoy it, couldn't release, not just because I'd made a promise to her, but because watching her broke my heart.

Finally, she slumped forward onto me, her head on

my shoulder, her body limp and weak even though her hips were still subtly grinding down on me.

With a hoarse voice, she whispered, "you're a miracle, Del. I can't believe—" She gasped and shuddered as another small orgasm rippled through her. "Through all that..." She lifted her head, her hair falling in a pale red curtain over her beautiful, speckled face, a thin veil, hiding nothing but making her all the more mysterious because of it.

"I've taken what I need," she murmured, even though I could tell from the desperate look in her eyes, she hadn't gotten what she truly needed: the return of our bond. "Your turn. Do what you will."

She moved in to press her lips to mine, her hair caught between us, but I didn't care. I kissed her all the same, wrapping my arms around her to press her amazing, lush body tight against me, savoring her hard, hungry lips against mine.

I was tempted to simply end this in that moment. Certainly, I was ready to, but now that it actually came to it, I hesitated. I'd let her take what she needed from me, let her use my body to distract her from the emptiness within her. Now I'd do a little taking of my own.

I carefully lifted her off me, making her gasp as I withdrew from her fully, and set her on the table beside us. She laid back, and I ran my hands up the insides of her thighs, opening her. Her entrance was swollen and wet, the perfect combination that would ensure a delicious, tight fit while still letting me push smoothly into her.

But instead of just plunging in, I teased her with my

fingers, sweeping her wetness over her clit, flicking and rubbing it, making her twitch and moan, building up a desire she thought she'd sated.

I didn't think she'd been expecting this. Indeed, I was caught off guard that I wasn't cock-deep inside her, desperate for my release. But I didn't want to just find my own pleasure, I wanted to give her more, wanted to show her even if our bond hadn't reformed that I'd still be there for her, still go to the end of the world and beyond to support her and bring her pleasure.

I slid two fingers inside her, curling them up to hit that magic spot that always made her cry out with need, and rubbed my thumb over her clit. She gasped and shuddered, writhing on the table, her hair splayed out behind her, her skin radiant with sweat, making her look like the goddess that I knew she was.

Another orgasm crashed through her, drawing a desperate, hoarse, "Yes!" from her lips, making me chuckle.

"More?" I purred, unable to help myself.

"Yes," she begged as if she hadn't already had enough, as if we were just getting started.

Keeping my fingers inside her, I knelt and replaced my thumb with my lips, sucking on that sensitive nub. Her fingers tangled in my hair, drawing me closer, and she bucked into my mouth, gasping and mewling at my ministrations.

I made her come again, hard and fast, her cry making my balls tighten, threatening an explosive release. I needed to get inside her. Now.

Before she was done trembling, I roughly pulled her

off the table, turned her around, and bent her forward, pressing her incredible breasts against the tabletop. Her legs were weak, so I held her hips, raising them until she was on her tip-toes. Even then I had to lower myself before I could find her opening with my cock.

She turned her head to the side, her golden gaze filled with a wild intensity meeting mine. "Yes, take me."

I thrust into her hard, stepping in as I brought her hips to mine. She cried her pleasure, her body already trembling again, another release building within her.

I withdrew and thrust again.

"Oh, yes," she cried, urging me on, and I thrust again and again. It was my turn to brand my heartache on her body, like she'd branded mine, and she was giving herself freely to me, like she always did.

I pounded into her, my strokes wild, frenzied and she heaved herself up on her arms and bucked her hips back, crashing our bodies together, trying to fill the emptiness inside us.

"Oh, gods!" Her head thrashed from side to side and her body started to tense with another orgasm.

I wrapped an arm under her chest and jerked her up, my pace frantic. I couldn't get deep enough, couldn't reach the part of her soul that would connect us again.

With a roar, I furiously thrust until I exploded inside her and her muscles clenched around me as she let out a wordless cry, shudders wracking her body just as shudders wracked mine.

We stayed that way, locked together in pleasure and soul-throbbing pain for a long moment. Then I released her, and she sagged on the table with a faint, tired smile.

I didn't want to take myself out of her. I wanted to stay within her forever and being connected like we were was our only way now. But eventually I withdrew from her, collapsed onto a chair, breathing hard, and pulled her into my arms.

My throat tightened with grief I refused to show her. Not after she so passionately made love to me. Gods, even with all of that the bond hadn't been restored. We'd shared a moment unlike anything I'd ever known and that hadn't done it.

Well, cursed crows! What was it going to take?

I held her, unwilling to let her go until she started shivering and had to get dressed. She took another long sip on the bottle of alcohol, then I helped her to a long, plush couch, where she collapsed and fell, almost instantly, into a fitful sleep.

I sighed, watching her, my chest aching. We were broken and neither of us knew how to put the pieces back together. At least not yet. Apparently, sex on a level beyond reason wasn't the answer.

I put my clothes back on and a little while later, Janice returned. I was leaning against the marble counters in the extravagantly large kitchen, not sure what to do, when she found me.

"You two have been quiet for a while, so I thought it safe to return," she said, pouring herself another drink.

"You could hear us? I thought you said this was a large house." It was certainly larger than most I'd seen in this world or my own—excluding the palace I'd grown up in.

"Oh, it is, but... wow. Annie is ungodly loud. I almost

thought you were torturing her for some of that, except most torture victims aren't yelling out those sorts of things." She downed half of what was in her glass then lifted the bottle to look at it. "I eventually found the wine cellar and that worked to block you two out... mostly. I think once I'm done with this bottle, I'll grab a few bottles from down there."

"You're just going to drink yourself into oblivion?" I asked, a bit worried for her.

"Yep. Seems like the right thing to do after one sprouts wings." She nodded, pain and confusion swirling in her eyes.

I'd seen the moment when those expansive golden-hued wings had burst forth. Even I'd been surprised. This woman, who'd thought herself a normal person from this world, must have been even more shocked, and I couldn't imagine what she must have felt.

Well, actually, perhaps it was like me discovering my water powers. Though that had come as a slow revelation, a creeping feeling and testing of abilities. So, no, it probably wasn't the same.

"Perhaps your wings could be seen as a gift?" I offered tentatively. "Now you can fly. Isn't that... something..." I didn't quite know how to finish that since I hated the sensation of flying myself.

"Oh, it's something all right." She downed the rest of the amber liquid and filled her glass again. The bottle was nearly empty now. "Yeah, sure, flying would be great. Too bad I have to do it topless and flash my tits at the world when I do. That's an amazing side effect." She rolled her eyes at me, her expression and tone sour.

I hadn't noted anything wrong with her breasts, but then, it did seem like the people of this world were a lot more body-conscious than those of mine. They insisted on covering themselves. I knew that was partly because it was ungodly cold here, but even inside they covered up as well, which suggested a certain shame perhaps about their bodies? Something I didn't fully understand.

She took a sip from her glass. "You have powers, right? How did you feel when you got them?"

"Amazing, confused, curious," I said, thinking back. "But mine didn't show up as... forcefully as yours and aren't as visibly obvious either."

"Remind me what you can do?" she said.

I pointed at the bottle she held and made the little remaining liquid within stream up and into my mouth, then I drank it down, savoring the invigorating burn as it rushed down my throat. "I can manipulate water."

She nodded, looking at the empty bottle. "Neat." Then she emptied the rest of her glass.

I was a bit shocked when she then threw the empty bottle across the room to shatter against a bank of cabinets on the far wall.

She quirked a smile at the random violence, then pushed off from where she'd been leaning against the counter. "If you need me, follow the smell of wine and confused self-loathing." Then she was gone.

This day wasn't going well.

As much as I wanted to curl up on the couch with Annie, there wasn't a lot of room for the both of us and my soul ached at the thought of being so close to her and yet not having her bond, so I found a room with a large bed and fell onto it, instead.

Outside, darkness was closing in, while despair was closing in inside me, and I hoped a night's sleep would help.

But a part of me said nothing would be right until Annie and I were bonded again.

And I didn't even know if that was possible.

I slept fitfully and woke groggy, feeling like I'd barely slept at all. Annie had introduced me to a wonderful—if bitter—drink called coffee, and I staggered down to the kitchen to see if I could find and attempt to make some.

Annie was still asleep on the couch and Janice was nowhere to be seen.

In a moment of worry for Janice, and uncertain if perhaps she might have drunk herself to death, I put off making coffee and searched the house for a while.

I found her passed out on a couch in a large room on the lower of two subterranean levels. Next to her sat a table with several open bottles, some of which had only a little wine missing, others of which were near to empty.

Gods.

I checked her life-beat at her neck.

It was strong.

It seemed the woman had a significant tolerance for alcohol and was still alive. Although I suspected she'd regret that when she finally woke.

She shifted at my touch, but didn't wake, and began snoring, so I left her there. Until Annie was awake, we wouldn't need Janice to help us come up with a rescue plan, and I wasn't going to wake Annie. She'd looked as broken as I felt last night, and I hoped that sleep was a reprieve from that heartache.

Back in the kitchen, I fumbled around, finding supplies for coffee, then making some. The first three attempts were awful, but the fourth was drinkable.

With that made, I stood with a steaming mug of the stuff, staring out a kitchen window at the frozen landscape beyond, and pondered what we should do next. We couldn't stay in this mansion forever, and we had to save the others—if they were even still alive. Gods, I hoped they were still alive. And once everyone was safe, we needed to find a way to get our bond with Annie back.

If that was possible.

A creeping doubt within me left black seeds of uncertainty that twisted around my heart.

We'd been as close as any two people could be last night and that hadn't done a thing. Though, to be fair, sex, even great sex, never was worthy of a bond in my world. It was only the intimacy of the touch of the lips that made it happen. Except that hadn't worked.

Perhaps we needed to return to my world to find out more about bonding? Someone had to know other ways to do it.

And the more I pondered that thought, the more going to my world made sense. Perhaps I could return to Galniosia and recruit some help to save the guys. My mother wouldn't like it, but to Hades with her.

Set on this course... I just had to wait for my companions to rouse themselves.

Annie was the first, sleepily and slowly swaying into the kitchen, her eyes still half closed. "Coffee?"

I nodded.

She held out her hands, her fingers making little grasping motions. "Coffee."

I poured her a cup and handed it over. She cradled the mug in both hands, sipping the dark liquid, then stumbled to a chair at the table and sagged down.

After another sip, she glanced at the table and the empty chair beside her—the chair where we'd made love—and a stunning blush seeped across her cheeks.

"Thank you for yesterday. That was…" Her face fell as she looked down at the floor. "It made me forget everything for a moment. A moment away from the horrid mess that's now my life."

"I had a thought," I said softly. She looked up, raising a brow in question. "We go back to my world. Perhaps there's someone there who knows more about how the bond works. Also, I might be able to recruit some of my people to return with us and help us get the others out of Hera's clutches."

Annie's face turned stony at the mention of Hera and she nodded stiffly.

"Good morning all!" Janice said, chipper and bright eyed as she strode into the kitchen. "I haven't slept— well passed out that well in ages!" She came over and poured herself some coffee, stunning me with her perky demeanor. I was expecting a half-alive half-awake mess of a woman that Annie would need to heal.

"You drink hard," I murmured.

She turned to me, sipping her coffee. "Yeah, my father got us started early and I had three brothers who liked to have drinking contests. I can drink any man under the table."

After last night, I had no doubt.

"We're going to go to my world," I said, and explained the plan I'd come up with.

She nodded, not even hesitating at the suggestion. "Wings yesterday, seeing a new world today, sure. Why the hell not?"

"You seem to have accepted the change... well?" I wasn't sure, given how she'd acted the previous day, if she had, or if she was on the verge of falling apart.

"A night of hard drinking often puts things in perspective for me. Well... first it puts things *way* out of perspective, but I think that helps to get it back to the right spot by the next day."

I supposed that made sense.

"Shall we be off then?" I looked at my two companions: Chipper Janice and hard, cold, heartbroken Annie. Gods, I wished there was something I could do to get Annie out of the depression she was in. But I suspected that wouldn't happen until she and I had bonded again, proving to both of us it was possible.

And I really hoped it was possible. It had to be.

CHAPTER 4

HYPERION

HERA KNEW THINGS. THINGS EVEN I DIDN'T KNOW ABOUT myself and my species. Strapped, face down to some hard table, arms and legs outspread, she'd known some way to make my wings come out and keep them from disappearing. Now she was painfully plucking my feathers, gleefully giggling. She hadn't asked any questions, hadn't wanted to know anything about us or Annie. This was torture just for fun apparently.

I'd held out as long as I could before I'd started screaming. It wasn't even the pain—though that was part of it—it wasn't even the thought of not being able to fly. *Erinai* molted, like any bird, but it happened in a measured, symmetrical way so we could retain our balance. Hera seemed to know this and was tearing the feathers only from one side. I'd be horribly disfigured and unbalanced until they regrew, and that could take up to six months. But it was the thought I wouldn't be able to fly with Annie for that long, which made me terrified that maybe I wouldn't be able to be with Annie at all, ever again.

That she was already gone.

I'd seen Hera throw her out of the building and I couldn't feel her inside me. My soul was empty, missing Annie's, and I had no idea if our connection would grow back like my essential feathers would.

Finished with the wing, Hera went to a table and grabbed a small knife, then she returned and began running it lightly over my back. She was never consistent, never the same pressure or duration, but always enough to hurt, and she made me agonize over where she'd carve into next.

"I can't recall," she said casually. "In your world do they have such a thing as 'death by a thousand cuts?'"

I grunted in response, my teeth clenched. I hoped she'd take it as a curse against her, but she didn't even seem to notice.

"Oh, it doesn't matter. I think I'll still enjoy explaining it to you. I have a very steady hand, you see. Half these cuts haven't even completely broken the skin. They're just for the pain. But the rest, well, they are shallow enough that they'll only bleed a little. You won't lose copious amounts of blood and die quickly. No, the whole point of 'death by a thousand cuts' is to make it so deliciously slow. Just a little blood here and there, and a lot of pain in between." She laughed and began humming to herself.

It was a delirious amount of time later when she spoke again. "How's that wing feeling?"

The haze of pain, which seemed to be everywhere, suddenly blossomed specifically at the base of the tattered wing as she dug the knife into my back. "If you want, I can cut the whole thing off... Would you like that? It's going to take some time for those feathers to return. Perhaps it would be better if you didn't have the wing at all?"

Gods, no! I bit the inside of my mouth, before I cried out. That was what she wanted. If she cut off my wing it would be permanently gone. I wouldn't be able to shed it and regrow it, I'd be flightless forever.

"I'll take that as a yes," she said and began digging in around that area, still using that small knife, taking ages to finally rip it free, and making me black out...

I came to, agony screaming through my back, molten fire burning where my wing came from my back— where it *used* to come from my back. My throat tightened, my gaze landing on my wing lying on the floor, dropped in my line of sight no doubt on purpose. Tears pricked my eyes and I couldn't fight them. I was never going to fly again. I was never going to be with Annie.

Hera was nowhere to be seen and I thanked all the gods for that. She'd love to hear my whimpers and see my tears, and I just didn't have it in me to hold it back.

My throat tightened even more with self-loathing at my selfishness. I was grateful Hera wasn't around, but that meant she was most likely with one of the others, and who knew what she was doing with them. I'd been raised in the military. I knew how to deal with pain. Admittedly what she'd done was well beyond anything I'd endured before, but still, I couldn't imagine her cutting on them and how they'd react, untrained and potentially less disciplined.

Except some soldier I was. I'd failed miserably in stopping Hera even with my power, and Annie and the others had paid a horrible price.

I heard a scream, faint in the distance and my jaw clenched harder.

I had to focus. While she wasn't around was my best chance to escape.

I heaved against my restraints, but they were too tight and I was weak from Hera's ministrations. My body —well everything on my back, except my other wing, pristine and untouched as it was—hurt beyond anything I'd ever felt before. Lines of fire crisscrossed all the way from my shoulders, over my buttocks and down my legs.

Still. I had to try. I couldn't think about the pain or about how tired I was, I had to keep trying to get away, for myself, for the others.

For Annie.

Oh gods, I couldn't think about that. I had to hope Del —who'd gone over the balcony after her—had saved her. She couldn't be dead. She just couldn't be!

Focus.

I was a soldier. I had to do something. I *could* do something.

I wrenched and twisted, sending agony through my body, making the thick leather straps dig into my wrists and ankles, and the one around my neck tighten, choking me.

Hera, whether out of ignorance or deliberate malice, hadn't told me what had happened to Annie. Out of all of Hera's tortures, that one hurt the most, eating at my heart as the emptiness of our missing bond sank deep and cold inside me.

I'd woken from my stupor in time to see her flying out the window. I'd leaped to my feet and tried to go after her, but Hera had seized me with her wind and howled with laughter as I heaved and screamed, knowing my mate was plummeting to her death.

Except I had to believe she was alive, no matter what the emptiness inside me was saying. Because if she wasn't, then I might as well just give into the pain and torture and die, too. I didn't want to live without her. I couldn't.

No. She couldn't be dead. She just couldn't be. And if she was alive, then she was out there, trying to figure out a way to free me and the others. With Del to help her, because he'd never leave her. And if she was alive and coming for me, then she'd be able to heal me. All the pain, the loss of the wing, it would mean nothing. I'd be whole again, in body and soul, as soon as she found us.

Agony screamed through my wing-socket and I jerked, my eyes snapping open, as someone—Hera— giggled. I wasn't sure when she'd returned and I had to assume I'd blacked out again.

"Fall asleep did we? Can't have that," Hera snarled, digging a finger around in the wound where my wing had been before grabbing her small knife and slicing into my skin again.

I gritted my teeth, fighting my scream and failing, panting through the agony.

I had to endure.

I would.

Annie was alive. The emptiness in my chest didn't mean she was dead.

She was alive.

She had to be.

Please.

CHAPTER 5

JANICE WATCHED DEL AND I STRIP OFF OUR CLOTHES AND raised her eyebrows at us. "You two aren't going to go at it like bunnies again, are you?" she asked.

We were in the other world, the one Hera had named... I couldn't remember what she'd named it and didn't want to think about her. I didn't want to think about anything to do with that woman right now or I knew I'd collapse into a puddle and wouldn't be able to stop sobbing.

I mentally focused on the wall I'd tried to build around my heart and concentrated on that. If I thought about anything else, about how the others could be dead, or how Hera could be torturing them—which, horrifically was the better of the two options—I'd break into a million pieces and wouldn't be able to save them.

And I *had* to save them.

Because they *were* alive.

"This is just the local dress," I said casually. "In that

the local dress is nothing. Everyone is naked here, no religiously imposed moral sensibilities, just bodies of all shapes and sizes and everything hanging out. It's really quite liberating once you get used to it." Not that I was feeling particularly liberated at the moment, but I'd also been too warm in my winter clothes. "Also it's damn hot here and wearing nothing is a lot more comfortable."

"Aren't you afraid you'll burn?" Janice asked. "Isn't that a thing with redheads and all that pale skin of yours?"

"Ah, good point. You should probably keep something on. You might burn," I replied. "But I won't. Not with my healing powers. I guess, to that point, I can heal you if you burn too, so it's up to you what you want to wear.

I caught Janice's gaze drifting over to Del and his magnificent body. I had to smile just a bit at the remembrance of our oh-so-incredible sex yesterday, but the small happiness didn't last as the aching emptiness of my missing bonds flooded back in.

Del and I stashed our clothes in a cubby in the rocks near the large black rock where the gate to my world was, and Janice, after a moment, shrugged and stripped as well.

"When in Rome and all that..." she said.

"I'm going to head home," Del said. "There are no huphelopoids here so you can't come. Are you going to be all right alone... with Janice?"

"Don't worry about me." I pursed my lips, realizing how stupid an expression that was. "Fuck it, worry about me. I'm worried as hell about you and the other guys, so yeah, whatever. But, yes, I'll be fine. We'll head into Masia and see if we can't recruit some help from there as well. It's not like I didn't cure the entire town... however long ago." I'd lost track of time entirely and it oddly felt like both a lifetime ago and just yesterday that I'd saved most of the village.

"True," he replied. "Hopefully they'll be willing to help." He bent down and gave me a soft, tender kiss, his lips brushing mine and I felt...

My pulse skipped a beat.

I felt *something* at that contact, a stirring deep within me. Except if it was something to do with our bond, it didn't go further than that faint, aching stirring.

And perhaps it had been my imagination, my desperate desire to be with Del again, to fill the void within me.

"I'll be back as soon as I can," he said.

I nodded. "I know. I love you."

"I love you, too." He wrapped his arms around me, holding me instead of leaving, not moving for a long time.

"It's okay," I murmured against his chest. "I'm not going to break. Go."

He brushed his lips against mine again then turned and ran for the waves, splashing into the surf then diving in—suddenly having his fish's tail again—and was gone into the blue-green waters.

"And... he's a mermaid," Janice said. "Of course he is."

I turned back to her. She'd taken off everything except her underwear, including her bra—although if I recalled correctly, she'd lost her bra along with her shirt when her wings had appeared. She was a very fit woman with a beautiful tanned complexion that was all natural and meant she didn't burn in a heartbeat like I did... like I *used* to. Still, I was just a tad jealous of her sleek physique. But then, I was the one with a harem of hunky men, not her, so... yeah.

"Ready?" I asked.

"Yeah. Although I couldn't seem to make myself do the Full Monty, not on my first time."

"You didn't have to do that much, if you didn't want to," I said and started walking toward the town sitting almost out of sight at the end of the beach. "Last time I was here, I was in a t-shirt and shorts. No, that wasn't the last time, that was the time before... or was it? Well one time at least."

"Oh. Well I'd be fine with this and a bra, if I had one, but it got ruined when my wings came out. So... this will do."

I didn't even attempt to offer her my bra. I was larger than she was in that area and it wouldn't have worked well and I was afraid it would have just made the situation more awkward.

We hiked across the sand toward Masia, the sun, a wonderful heat, seeping into my skin, but it was unable to penetrate the dread for my guys and my missing bonds that churned in my gut and chilled my soul.

A part of me still didn't know how everything had gone so wrong, while the rest of me tried to shove those thoughts aside. I'd made a choice and even if it had turned into a disaster, I still knew in my heart it was the right decision... well, maybe not entirely right because we'd had our asses handed to us, but someone had to have done it. Someone had needed to stand up to Hera and stop her, and now that someone needed to pull up her big girl panties, get her guys back, and figure out how not to lose the next time.

And so long as I kept that thought in mind, maybe I wouldn't crumble into a sobbing heap.

About half an hour later, we reached Masia. The first time I saw the village, I hadn't thought it was much. The guys had called it a town, but it wasn't much more than a collection of shacks of varying sizes, and a dirt road that led from a long, narrow dock to a public square with a dozen vendors selling their wares.

On that first glance, I'd guess there were maybe a couple hundred people living in Masia and now it seemed like every one of them knew about me, if not by sight, then by name. People nodded their respect to me in passing, some even came up and gave me gifts of food or flowers, making me feel like I was some kind of hero.

It was a lot to take in, and from the size of Janice's eyes, it was even more for her to take in.

"The people are..." Janice whispered, her gaze jumping from a woman with horse legs like Aethan's to an enormous cyclops. "They're not..."

"Human? Yeah, you get used to it after a while." Well, to be fair, I still wasn't entirely used to it. Seeing a minotaur or centaur or a gaggle of girls with skin as brightly colored and varied as wildflowers was still just a bit odd for me.

"Why is everyone so— How do they know you?"

"I healed the village, well most of it, when that plague guy came through here."

"He was here too? Not just on earth?"

"Yep, he was from our world initially, but got his powers here. I think anyone who can travel between the worlds, like him and me, they get powers here."

"Ohhhhh..." she said, the word drawn out before fading away. "I feel like there's so much I don't know. There's so much everybody on earth doesn't know. There's a whole other world and no one knows about it. How's that possible?"

"I'm still a little fuzzy on that myself, but from what I understand, only certain people from our side can open the gates. Also, apparently, there are fewer gates then there used to be, and as you saw, they're well hidden. So, it would take an incredible coincidence for someone with the power to open a gate to find one and open it."

"Like you did?" she replied. "How did that happen anyway?"

"I..." I grimaced. I'd just said it would take an incredible coincidence, and it had. What were the chances I'd slip on some ice and fall through that wall? What were the chances I'd have dropped my phone and it would have been kicked into that alley?

Perhaps me going through the gate had been somehow fated. "Hunh..."

"What?"

"Ah... nothing. Yeah, it was very coincidental. I dropped my phone, and someone kicked it into that alley. I followed it in there, slipped on a patch of ice, and fell through the wall."

"Wow, really?"

"Yeah."

"That's some next level coincidence. If I didn't know better, I'd say it was meant to be," Janice said.

Which was exactly what I'd been thinking.

I pushed open the door to the cantina and we entered the dark, slightly cooler interior. There was still a crowd inside of—now that I wasn't suffering from heat stroke and could get a better look at them—people who looked rough around the edges, like this was the seediest bar in Masia... even though I had a feeling it was the *only* bar in Masia. But the crowd wasn't nearly as large as before, reminding me that while I'd saved much of the village, I hadn't saved everyone.

The man behind the bar had large horns curling out the side of his head, like a ram, squarish eyes, and I assumed his legs were goat like. He was like the healer-woman who'd been tending the sick-camp that first time I'd been here.

"Hello good sir, do you know who I am?" I asked, leaning on the bar.

"You are Anichambers, the healer woman, savior of Masia." The way he said my name, all running together like one word, was odd, but it was how most of the people in the village had already addressed me so I didn't correct him—trying to change an entire village was a battle I didn't want to bother with, not right now.

"Yep, I am, and now I need some assistance. Do you think some of the people here in the cantina, or the village in general, would be willing to help me?"

He bobbed his head vigorously. "Of course. You only have to ask."

"Good. I'll start with the people here. Mind if I stand on your bar?"

He quirked a brow, but waved a hand for me to go ahead, and I hopped up on the bar.

"Hey," I shouted to the assembled crowd.

All eyes turned to me and a part of me was suddenly acutely aware that I was naked and standing on a bar for everyone to see. It seemed like something a younger— and very drunk—version of myself might have done, but here I was, and I didn't feel particularly ashamed or self-conscious. I was even feeling a little liberated.

"I'm Annie Chambers." I separated the words just enough to satisfy me, but also made it sound like the name these people knew me by. "And I need some help. I'm a great healer, but there are some things I can't do, and I'm going to need some strong and willing people to assist me."

A chorus of shouts and cries went up, people offering to help without even knowing what I was asking. Hands shot up in the air, waving at me, and a small part of me heaved a sigh of relief. Sure, I'd helped save the village and my welcome back to Masia had been warm, but that didn't mean they'd want to help me.

But then guilt twisted in my stomach. I had to say more, had to make the situation clear. I didn't want to be responsible for more people getting hurt, but I wasn't going to be able to free my guys—because they were alive, God damn it—without help.

"Now you should know, this is a very, *very* dangerous

mission." I stressed these words and the cries quieted down and some of the hands withdrew. "In fact, I won't lie to you. You'll be going to save some of your own people who've been taken prisoner by a god. Well a goddess, actually. Hera."

Silence fell over the crowd. There were a few gasps and whispered words. The ones I heard the most were: 'goddess' and 'Hera.'

"Three of my friends, men who used to frequent this very cantina from time to time, are in trouble." *Please, gods, let them just be in trouble and not dead.* "They are being held in a..." High rise wasn't a word they'd know. "Fortress?" That seemed to get some recognition. "A well-fortified tower. There will be many people with weapons, very advanced... god weapons." How else could I explain guns?

"God weapons?" Janice asked, whispering.

"These people have no idea what a gun is," I whispered back to her.

"Ah, right. Okay."

"There's a good chance those who come with me will be hurt, perhaps killed," I said, turning back to the crowd. "I can heal wounds, but I can't bring someone back from the dead."

Although... I'd never actually tried to bring someone back from the dead. Maybe I could? Wouldn't that be something! Fuck. Best to keep things limited and scary for this group though. As much as I wanted their help, *needed* it, I didn't want any of them agreeing to go with us without knowing all the risks.

"I'm a healer, not a warrior. I don't want to send

anyone into danger," I continued. "But I'm going either way and I could really use some help. If you're willing, meet me down by the docks at sunset today. And spread the word around the town if you think anyone might be interested." I took a long moment then to scan the crowd, moving from face to face of as many as I could see. Such a variety of people. A part of me hoped they wouldn't come. They didn't deserve to be hurt for my crazy quest, but another part prayed they would. Because I wouldn't be able to free my guys without help. Lots of help.

I drew in another breath, uncertain how to finish and decided, "Thank you," was simple and probably all I needed. Then I hopped down off the bar.

"Wow, that was impressive." Janice said, seeming a bit star-struck herself. "Where did you learn to speak like that?"

"Like what?"

"So... moving."

"Really? That was moving?"

"Yeah."

"Oh..." Hunh. "I just said what I wanted to." But it occurred to me then that I was riled up. I was vibrating with energy. I desperately needed to get my guys back and find some way to rebond with them. It was imperative for me. Perhaps that had come out through my words.

"So," Janice asked, as we stepped out of the cantina onto the dusty, hard-packed dirt street in the center of the village. "What now?"

"We wait for sunset. Care to walk along the beach and get a tan?"

She smiled and gave a slight nod. There was an odd look in her eyes, a reappraisal of me perhaps? I couldn't quite tell. She didn't elaborate, and it didn't look like she wanted to talk about it. It didn't look like she wanted to talk at all, like she had as many fearful and confused thoughts rushing through her head as I did.

CHAPTER 6

My family had been surprised to see me back so soon, and my sister, Poseia, had had a lot of questions. I'd told her they'd all be answered at the formal hearing, then I'd requested that hearing, and now stood once again before my whole family. My mother and father were on their thrones, flanked by Poseia and Luarnon, and Mother didn't look happy at all. Of course, the last time I'd been there, she'd disowned me and kicked me out of the kingdom, so I was already prepared for a less than warm welcome from her.

"You renounce your throne then return so quickly to ask something of us?" my mother demanded. "Of course you have. You could never do anything on your own."

I tried to ignore her bitter tone, but it struck a nerve I'd been trying to not think about. Even with my closest friends and my mate who was as powerful as a goddess, we still hadn't been able to stand up against Hera. That failure was just more proof that I was hopeless at everything.

But I couldn't leave the others to Hera. Even if we hadn't all bonded with Annie, I wouldn't have left them behind. I'd do anything to save them and if that meant humbling myself to my mother, then so be it.

"Hanea, stop it," my father said sternly. I wasn't used to him standing up to her like that. It was a new side of him that I was grateful was making an appearance. Hopefully with his help, I'd be able to convince my mother to give us an army. "Let the boy speak." He nodded at me, indicating I should make my request.

I sucked in a steadying breath, trying to still my whirling thoughts and fears. I had to word this just right or my mother and everyone else wouldn't listen.

"Your majesties," I said with a stiff and formal bow to both of them. That got a raised brow from my mother. Like always, I couldn't tell if that was good: curiosity, or bad: on the verge of a tongue-lashing. "I've come as a citizen of Galniosia, who was once a royal. I gave up my right to the crown and with it any power I might hold over this kingdom. I know that I have little or no power here."

"No power is right," my mother huffed.

I nodded to her, acknowledging this. "As you say." Here came the hard part... the truth. I turned my attention to Poseia who knew about our plans to defeat Hera with a look that I hoped said: I may need your help now, sister. "To fully explain my request of the crown, I need to give a little history. It may be hard to understand, as it involves things I, and all of us, once thought impossible. I hope you'll listen with an open mind."

Poseia shook her head, her eyes sad, telling me I'd

already erred somewhere, and I slid my gaze back to my mother who wore a haughty look of 'he's going to make up some story.' Damn, I'd already lost her.

But I still had my father. He still looked interested, if concerned, and maybe with his new found command, he'd be enough to give me the help I needed.

"As you know, eight years ago, I took the place of the functionary you were sending as emissary to the lands above as part of The Treaty of Eronatus. Since then, I have happily taken on that duty and represented Galniosia in the meeting of emissaries." Everyone seemed to be following so far. "Those three men, with whom I met, became good friends of mine. In many ways they are like a second family to me." I looked long and hard at my mother for this next bit. Since I'd already lost her, it wouldn't hurt to get in a jab. "They accepted me for who I was, no conditions, just brotherly love."

Mother scowled and Father shot her a dark look, stopping whatever jab she was going to send back.

"At our last meeting of emissaries, there was an interruption. A strange woman came to Masia and used powers of healing, true healing, to eradicate a plague the town had been suffering." That was an amalgamation of several events into one, but it seemed a reasonable summary for the sake of expediency. Everyone except my mother looked surprised, raising eyebrows or sitting forward. "That woman was the one I brought to visit the last time I was here."

"The *heliai*?" Luarnon said.

I nodded. "Yes... but she's not *heliai*. And here begins

the more... fantastical part of my tale, though I swear to you that every word is true."

A scoff from my mother. The others—except Poseia—looked dubious.

"Annie, this healer-woman, is from another world. She isn't *heliai*. She's human."

"Human!" Mother shot up from her throne, suddenly and shockingly enraged, which was something I hadn't expected at all.

I didn't think anyone knew what a human was. But I'd forgotten that my mother was raised from childhood to be the perfect queen. She'd been taken in by my grandmother, my father's mother, and trained in every way. She was well educated, perhaps more so than my father.

"Humans are what drove us from the paradise oceans. They multiplied rapidly and when there was no room for them and our kind, they and the gods drove us from paradise!"

They drove us from paradise? From Annie's world?

But then, I did recall hearing something like that... but where...?

Hera! I tried not to tense my jaw at the memory of listening to Annie and Hera talk over the *fone* while returning from the hospital. It had been when Annie had first met that horrid woman, going with her in that odd stretched out car, while us guys had followed behind. Hera had mentioned something—though we'd barely been able to hear her—about how in her time people had moved freely between the two worlds.

It seemed that most in this world didn't remember or

believed it to be a myth, but my mother still knew the truth.

Although, if I really thought about it, while Annie's world seemed more advanced, I wouldn't have called it paradise. My world was much more like a paradise. Annie had even said as much.

"Annie is a good person. She healed the entire town of Masia even though it brought her to the brink of death." That might have been a bit of an exaggeration, but not by much. She'd worked until she'd passed out and had remained unconscious for hours. "Yes, humans can be petty and cruel and evil, but they certainly aren't the only ones."

I shot a hard look at my mother. I knew it was foolish. I shouldn't have baited her any more than I already had, but I couldn't help myself.

Poseia raised a hand to her forehead and gave me a look which said, 'you've messed up. Good luck getting help now.'

Yeah, that might have been a bit heavy handed.

"Annie's heritage is beside the point," I continued. "It's my friends—"

"She's human. That's not beside the point!" My mother proclaimed. "She's—"

"A good woman!" I yelled back. I could yell over her just as easily. "And if you want to condemn me or her, that's fine, but by all the gods, sit down and listen to my whole story first. Then you can banish me, if that's what you want!"

Mother's eyes went wide with the shock that I'd spoke back to her so forcefully, something I'd never done before. I'd been snide, sullen, and just plain ignored her, but I'd never spoken back before.

She blinked, an odd look on her face. I had no idea what she was thinking, but some of the tension left her shoulders and she drifted back down onto her throne.

"Tell your story then," she replied, her tone soft and filled with malice.

By Hades, it looked like I'd done it now.

Except my friends were in danger—if they were still alive—and I couldn't back down. I needed help.

I bit the inside of my cheek. I shouldn't have lost my temper. I wasn't sure why I had. My mother just made me so angry sometimes.

I drew in a long breath, fighting to calm myself.

"My friends, those I consider to be like a second family. They are in paradise, as you call Annie's world. They went there with myself and Annie to try to get rid of Hera, a human— yes a *human*, not a god, although she has many powers which makes her akin to one," I said. "We failed in our first attempt and my friends were captured. I've come to ask for the assistance of Galniosia to free them from the hold of this horrible woman and to liberate our people and the people of the paradise world."

"Is that all?" mother asked sharply.

It wasn't, but I wasn't going to ask mother about rebonding with Annie. That would be a question for Umandra, the Royal Archivist, assuming I wasn't run out of the palace first. I didn't think my father would let that happen, but given my mother's temper, who knew. "Yes."

Mother rose again, this time stately and calm. "You

seek the aid of our people, our soldiers, to free your friends?"

"Yes." And here came the refusal.

"You, who have no say here, who have shirked all responsibility? You want our people to go and die for some land-dwellers? Do you think I care anything for your friends? They're not tritons!" Her voice had risen with each word to a culminating yell by the end.

I looked at my father, whose expression was tired and worn.

"Don't look at him! We rule this kingdom together. A call to war such as this would need the unity of the king and queen. If I say no, then that's the end of it," she snarled.

My father nodded slowly, but then he, too, rose. "I think perhaps there may be more to consider, my queen," he said stoically.

"There isn't," she huffed.

"Just sit down and listen, Hanea!" my father snapped, shocking me.

He'd never taken that tone with my mother before and she looked at him, her jaw tense, muscles twitching, and sat down slowly. "Listen? To what?"

My father turned to me. "Tell us of this Hera? What is she like? Why did you try to get rid of her?"

"She infected hundreds of people in this world and the other world with a horrible plague, a disease that could have scoured both our worlds. And it's only because of Annie that both worlds were cleansed of it."

My father frowned. "Why did Hera do this?"

"That I do not know." I saw the wicked smile starting

to spread on my mother's face as if she thought she'd won. "But that's exactly what makes her truly dangerous," I added.

My mother's eyes narrowed.

"In the other world she's powerful, more powerful than all of the kings and rulers of our islands combined. She's beyond the laws of both worlds and can do anything she likes," I said. "We don't know what she's planning, but someone who would casually infect thousands of people for any reason, is someone I wouldn't want around. Yes, she's in the other world right now, but what if she decided to turn her attention here? What would we do then? Our kingdoms are divided. She'd easily walk over each of our territories and take us one by one."

"We're beneath the waves, she wouldn't be able to—"

"Are you certain of that mother?" I countered quickly.

My mother opened her mouth then snapped it shut. She wasn't a pleasant woman, but she wasn't foolish, and I could practically see her mind going over all the possibilities, coming to the realization that she didn't know if our kingdom was safe or not.

"What makes her dangerous is that she's powerful and unchecked, and we have no clue what she's going to do with all that power. She tried to start a plague in both our worlds just because she could. We were lucky that Annie managed to stop it, but we have to stop Hera before she does something worse, something we can't protect against."

My mother's expression grew even more grim, and

Poseia gave me a slight nod, telling me my argument was good and I might have actually won.

"We wouldn't be able to lend you many men," my father said, turning his attention to my mother.

Her scowl deepened. "A dozen. If Hera is going to attack, we need to be able to protect ourselves."

"A score," Father offered. "Better to stop her in paradise than on our boarder."

"Fine, a score, no more," my mother huffed as she turned her hard gaze on me. "And for every one of them that falls, you will owe this kingdom fifty pearls."

I raised my brows at that. That was a steep price. If only a couple men died, I'd be paying that off for years. If they all didn't make it back, my children's children would be repaying that debt.

"Hanea," my father said. "That's—"

"My final offer," she interrupted, turning her glare back to him. "Take it or leave it."

My father sighed and both he and my mother returned their attention to me.

"Well?" my father asked.

"Agreed," I said. I didn't have much choice. Hera needed to be stopped and I could only hope my mother's selfishness didn't put our kingdom and the rest of our world in danger.

Poseia raised a brow, her expression a mix of surprise and worry. Me agreeing to such horrible terms told her just how serious this situation was.

"Come, brother," she said. "I'll escort you to the court-yard to wait for your men."

"I'll gather your men," said my brother, Luarnon, who'd been silently watching the exchange.

He swam out the door behind the throne, while Poseia led me back out of the Hall of Light.

"Do you think we can go to the courtyard by way of the library?" I asked, keeping my voice low. "I need to ask Umandra a few questions."

"I'm not sure if she has more information about Hera," Poseia said, even as she turned down the hallway that would lead us to the library and the Royal Archivist.

I doubted Umandra would, and even if she did, all we had was legend and Hera was so much more than our legends. "I need information on bonds."

Poseia swished to a stop and grabbed my arm. "What's happened?"

My chest tightened. Everything had happened. The worst thing possible. And I was grateful my sister didn't immediately accuse me of being immature and trying to get out of my bond with Annie—not that I would have needed Umandra's help to leave a normal mating bond.

"My bond with Annie is— *was* deeper than just a normal bond. There was some kind of magic involved in our joining."

Poseia's eyes narrowed. "Was? Is Annie okay?"

No. None of us were. "She's alive and unharmed, but Hera broke our bond." I pressed a hand against my chest. The emptiness inside me was overwhelming, and I'd only lost one bond. I couldn't imagine how much Annie hurt.

And yet she was still pushing forward, still willing to fight. Which only proved how strong she was.

"I have to get our bond back," I said. I'd never leave

Annie, and I knew the others, once we'd rescued them, wouldn't either even without the bond, but I didn't want her to spend the rest of her life with a constant reminder that there should have been more between us.

"If anyone knows about this magical bond, Umandra would," Poseia said, resuming her course to the library.

Unfortunately, the aged librarian hadn't read anything about a bond being more than just a kiss on the lips that sealed a lifelong promise to be together. She knew nothing about the magic that had joined me and Annie and there was little in the library about something so mundane as non-magical mating bonds.

And if the information wasn't in the Library of Galniosia then it likely wasn't anywhere.

Which meant I didn't know how to fix our bond and I wasn't looking forward to telling Annie that.

CHAPTER 7

IT WAS AN ODD ASSORTMENT OF CREATURES WHO'D COME to join Janice and I on the sand near the long docks of Masia. There were three minotaurs, tall and broad, with their odd, bull-like horned heads and shaggy hooved feet, and two *panai*, which I'd come to know was the name for the people with the goat-like eyes, horns, and legs. A few feet away stood a satyr, with features like Aethan, and the same sort of horse-like mohawk mane of hair, and next to them a large woman—half a head taller than the minotaurs, but not as large as Keph—with only one central eye, a cyclops.

The five others were a variety of nymphs, two *epimelidai* with skin of mottled browns and greens, and an *oreadai* with skin of pale gray and soft white. The last two both had wings, but I was told weren't *erinai* like Rion. The one was a *nephelai*, with wings of gleaming silver, similar to Rion's snowy white wings, but the man's skin was also a pale silver-white, and the other winged man was an *aurai*, with wings of dappled gold.

Aurai was what Del had called Janice, and she kept glancing at the *aurai* man as if she wanted to talk to him but didn't have the courage. Which was kind of silly. A shy FBI agent. Who knew?

"Go talk to him," I said softly.

"What would I say? 'Hey there, I'm from another world, but I just found out I have wings like yours, we should talk?'"

"Those aren't the worst words. Why not try it?"

"He's from another world!" she insisted.

"So are the four men I fell in love with."

She glanced back at the *aurai* man who caught her look and gave him an awkward wave.

He smiled at her and nodded in return.

"An excellent start," I said, trying not to giggle. "Now how about trying words?"

"Maybe later," she huffed.

I snorted at her. For a tough FBI agent, it seemed Janice wasn't so aggressive in relationships. But I wasn't going to push. It was ultimately up to her, even if she just wanted to find out more about herself.

We had a full dozen men waiting—well ten men and two women, the cyclops and one of the minotaurs were female—and I had no clue how we were going to get them across Chicago to Hera's tower, looking like they did. But that was a problem for later.

"Thank you all for coming," I called out, and the group quieted, the soft hubbub of chatter dropping away. "Let me say again, this mission we're going on isn't going to be easy and your lives may be in danger. Are you sure you're willing to come with us?"

"We heard there may be pay in this for us?" the female minotaur said. "The three of us are mercenaries. We fight for gold."

Several others muttered similar things which seemed to suggest more than half the group thought they might get paid for this.

Hunh.

"I don't have anything to give you," I said honestly, because lying to a bunch of minotaurs was a terrible idea, and I could see that didn't go over well. "But we're going to fight a goddess. Any loot you can find is yours once the battle is done." I didn't know what Hera might have that these people would want, but it couldn't hurt to let them root around and take whatever they wanted. She was uber-rich after all and her apartment had been filled with expensive looking art and things.

That did catch their attention, both the part about fighting a god and the part about loot. A small group, including the minotaurs, still seemed hesitant however.

"There was mention of a god," the female minotaur huffed as if she didn't believe that. Guess she was the spokesperson for their party. "Tell us more. Which one?"

More? Well, that was fair.

"As you may know, I'm not like those here. I can heal, and that ability comes from the fact that I'm from another world. That world has many people, some of whom have abilities which make them like gods. Apparently, some of your gods may have come from my world long ago." I wasn't entirely sure about that part, but Hera had implied that all the Greek gods and goddesses had been her friends from my world. "We'll travel to my world to face one of these people with powers, who I believe you see as a god. Her name is Hera."

More muttering, but oddly not in fear as I might have thought. Instead it seemed eager.

"We're in," the minotaur called over. "It'll be good to test our mettle against a god, especially Hera. She was never good to our people."

Oh. Interesting. Well, that was fortunate.

"And the rest of you?"

The two *panai* were arguing with each other and the satyr looked hesitant. After a moment one of the *panai* stalked away with some words thrown back at us in a language I didn't understand. After a tremulous moment, the satyr followed, running off.

That brought us down to ten, but still more than I'd thought would have been willing.

Not bad.

But I'd give them one more out... because I wasn't sure my conscience could handle it if I was responsible for getting them killed.

"Are you certain you wish to come with us?" I pressed. "This is a very powerful woman, and she has many men guarding her. Their weapons are unlike anything you've seen before. I say again, this will be rough, some of you may be injured or die."

"You're doing a great job of selling this," Janice whispered, rolling her eyes at me.

"They need to know what they're getting into," I whispered back. "I want the risk to be clear."

There were a few more mutters, but no one else left.

Thank goodness.

"Then gather anything you might need for a long trip and meet back here. We're waiting on possibly some more support from the tritons."

Someone, the cyclops woman, scoffed at that, but I wasn't sure why she'd have that reaction.

A few left, but most stayed. It seemed they had everything they needed already. Perhaps they travelled light, though, I had to admit, this group was wearing more clothes than I'd seen in one place in this world. Although to be fair, it wasn't so much clothes as armor.

Then there was nothing else to do, so I sat on the edge of the dock. "Now we wait for Del and his reinforcements... hopefully."

Janice sank to the dock beside me, her gaze still on the group, her expression still shocked. I watched her eyeing them for a long moment, before she tilted her head curiously to one side and realization hit me.

"You're undressing them in your mind, aren't you?"

Her lips quirked in a smile. "It's strange. I've seen most of these folks in town—either this particular person or someone like them—and they were naked. But now that they're wearing things, I can't stop... It's fascinating."

It certainly was.

Though it lent credence to something one of the guys had said to me, that I got more alluring whenever I was dressed. Something about being a mystery, a tease. This new world was turning everything I thought on its head.

"And that *aurai* fellow, are you undressing him too?"

"Of course." Her gaze flicked to me, her smile increasing. "You've already got four hunky guys, leave me to my fantasies."

That was fair.

And that *aurai* man was handsome enough to spawn a few daydreams. He wasn't tall like my guys, though not small or short either. For my world, he'd have been average height, though in this crowd, he was taller than most except the minotaurs and the cyclops. And he was well filled out, with a thick, muscular chest under his heavy-looking plates of armor.

His shoulders were covered, but his upper arms were not and they were thick, the muscles bunching as he settled down, chatting with the *nephelai* next to him. He had a square jaw, piercing blue eyes, and long—yet somehow light and billowing—blond hair. He was Fabio, but with wings, which were folded behind him for the moment.

Hopefully he wasn't a complete jerk.

He glanced over at us again and smiled. I was fairly certain his eyes were more on Janice than me, and I gave a slight head tilt, indicating Janice. The man raised a brow, then nodded and rose, making his way over to us.

"Ah..." Janice said, stiffening as he approached.

"Just be yourself," I whispered, patting her shoulder and getting up to leave to give the two of them some privacy.

"Wait," she said, reaching for me.

I evaded her grasp. "He's not an enemy. Talk to him."

Except her eyes were wide as if she was actually panicking over talking with him.

"Hello?" the man said. "My name is Athanasios, though most call me Nasios or just Naz."

"I'm, ah... Janice."

"A pleasure," he said, and I turned away and walked down the long pier.

The dock stretched far into the water, as the shore was shallow here and I guessed larger boats wouldn't be able to get too close. There weren't any boats docked at the moment, and I strode out to the end, marveling at the beautiful teal waters. Soon, the sea would grow darker, changing color and reflecting the many vibrant hues of the imminent sunset, and while I knew it would be beautiful, I couldn't seem to feel excited for it. I wasn't sure I could be excited for anything, not with the emptiness in my soul.

"I hope you're having as much luck down there, as I am up here," I whispered.

"It wasn't easy, but I think I was lucky enough," Del said behind me.

Surprised, I spun, and there he was. He was wet, perhaps having just come out of the water, his blue-black hair, somehow still sexy, swept back and dripping. Just seeing those broad shoulders and wide chest, the strong arms, and sculpted abs leading down to that oh-my-gods-sized cock, made me weak in the knees. I leaped into his waiting arms. Even just having been away from him for one day had been far too long.

It was only once I was plastered to his wet body that I noticed his sister, Poseia, in the periphery of my vision, standing next to him.

Oh...

My initial awkwardness at seeing her was overridden by my desire and love for Del. With my legs and arms wrapped around him, I pressed close and kissed him long and full. Let his sister see us. There was equal passion in his kiss, and once again I felt something stir deep within me. I hoped, prayed, pleaded that it would turn into more, but it didn't, and I drew my lips away, curious and caught up in this odd sensation.

Del must have seen my curious confusion, and he set me down. "What is it?"

"Did you feel something just now when we kissed?"

Poseia gave a short laugh. "It sure looked like he was feeling most of you."

"Nothing other than all the wonderful things I'd expect to feel with you in my arms," he said, his eyes roaming over me and warming my insides. Suddenly I wanted to get him somewhere much more private.

But still... Odd.

He wasn't feeling anything special.

"What did you feel?" he asked.

I shrugged. "I don't know really. Something... deep within me. Something stirring."

"Do I need to leave you two alone for a while?" Poseia asked with a chuckle.

"No," we both said quickly. Then, once again speaking over each other, "Well, yes. But—"

All three of us laughed at that.

"But I was feeling more than just... that," I said to Del. "I mean, I do want to get you somewhere private and do all manner of unspeakable things with you, but this was something more, something deeper."

His expression darkened. "I wish I could say I felt the same, but I don't think I feel what you're feeling."

Yeah, this was more than just my love or lust for him, but if it was something related to bonding, I'd expect Del to be feeling it too. I knew—or maybe I just hoped—there was more to this feeling, but for now, I had no clue what it was.

A spike of laughter from down the docks caught my attention. I looked around Del to see Janice laughing at something Naz had said. She seemed much more relaxed with him now.

Good.

If only I was feeling so relaxed. This strange sensation within me had me perplexed and unsettled and worried that I'd never get my bonds back.

"I managed to get twenty men," Del said, changing the subject. "It seems you've had a bit of luck as well."

"Yes, ten men and women from the village."

"Women?" he asked.

Poseia slapped him. "We can fight as well as any man."

"Uh, yes, of course."

"And we strategize better than most men. That's why he brought me along," she added.

"That's why she insisted on coming," he said. "She thought we could use some help in figuring out our next step."

"We could, thank you," I said with a nod to the keen young woman. "Are you going to fight with us?"

"I'm flattered that you assumed I could, and I can, but no," she replied. "I'm terrified of what you two are about to do and not stupid enough to try it."

"That makes you smarter than both of us, I think."

She smiled at that, but there was a look of concern in her eyes, like she didn't want to lose her older brother.

Well, I didn't want to lose him either.

"We'd very much appreciate your help," I said. "I want to make sure we all come back alive and well."

"Indeed." Del released a heavy breath and grimaced.

I quirked a brow at that.

"Long story," he replied.

"Not really," Poseia said. "He agreed to pay an exorbitant sum back to my mother for every triton who falls in battle."

I raised my other brow.

He shrugged. "We needed the help. I had to agree."

Which was true. "Then, let's go have a chat and see if we can't ensure we all stay safe."

CHAPTER 8

ANNIE

AFTER JUST ONE EVENING WITH HER, I WAS FAIRLY CERTAIN Poseia was smarter than everyone else in our small army combined. The sheer amount of tactical knowledge in her head, and the ease with which she recalled it, was amazing. She also quickly assimilated what Janice told everyone about our human world and adapted plans on the fly when I was having trouble keeping up. Not that I was a tactical genius, or a tactical anything, really, but still, it was astounding.

Eventually it was just Janice and Poseia chatting away like old friends, planning our attack on Hera's tower in Chicago while of the rest of us tuned them out and settled down for the night.

"Your sister is amazing," I said, as Del gesture toward the beach, indicating he wanted to go for a walk. "So smart and friendly."

He laughed and I took his arm, letting him lead me away. "She got the best qualities of both my parents. Unlike me."

"Oh, I very much like your qualities," I said suggestively, waggling my eyebrows at him.

"And I yours," he purred back, echoing my innuendo.

After that, we walked in silence, hand in hand, wading through warm, soothing, ankle-deep water until we were a good distance from the others. Then, away from eyes and ears, standing in the pale light of a full moon and under a brilliant expanse of stars, he turned me to face him and stepped in close.

My heart pounded. I'd hoped he'd had more of a reason for wanting to get away than just stretching his legs and clearing his mind, and his hard erection, captured between us told me clearly I hadn't been wrong.

"I feel guilty doing this," he breathed, "having you all to myself, while the others..."

My heart lurched at the thought of my other guys being held by Hera—because, God damn it, they were alive. I wasn't even going to consider that they were dead. The trouble was, if they were alive, then they were probably in agony, and I wasn't sure if that was better.

"No," I said, my voice catching with those horrible thoughts. "We'll get them back and then they'll have all the time in the world with me. I'll take them for long walks on this beach, so don't feel guilty. Just... love me now." I swallowed hard. "Make me forget about everything for a moment. Free my heart so I have the strength to free them tomorrow. Please," I begged.

"Yes," he replied, his voice husky, and he lifted me. I wrapped my legs around his waist and our lips met, crushing together in a heated kiss.

He lifted me higher, kissing his way down to my

breasts, tasting them, teasing my nipples into tight buds, as the tip of his cock brushed against my opening. With a sigh, I gently rocked my hips, rubbing myself over him, teasing his length between my slick folds.

"Oh, yes." I let my head fall back and savored the heat growing inside me and his strong arms, holding me as if I was weightless.

He dragged his teeth over the tight bud of one aroused nipple, licking the tip before pulling back. "Have you ever coupled in the water before?"

I'd tried once, long ago, in a backyard pool. It had been stimulating at first, as my boyfriend at the time had stripped away the bits of my bikini, tossing them onto the patio. Then we'd played for a bit before he'd discarded his swimming trunks. But after that it had just gotten awkward as he'd tried to tread water and fuck at the same time. It had been good for him. But I hadn't gotten anything out of it.

That memory had soured me on the thought of sex in the water in general, but then again... Del was a triton. The water was his domain, and just like the sky was Rion's and having sex with him while flying had been incredible, I knew it would be just as incredible to have sex with Del in the water.

"Show me your world," I murmured. "Show me what sex with a triton is like."

"With pleasure," he chuckled and carried me into the water, my legs still hooked around his waist, his length still nestled between my folds, shifting with each step, teasing me in the most delicious way.

We headed farther and farther away from the shore.

The warm water took some of my weight, helping me float, while Del took the rest, his movements becoming more fluid as he switched from legs to his fish tale.

Which brought back the memory of the first time I'd seen him and his jaw-dropping erection, appearing from nowhere from his tail. I didn't think I'd ever forget how shocked and turned on I'd been.

Finally, when the fire from our camp was just a speck in the distance, he stopped and rocked his hips, sliding himself against me, the movement slow and sensual, his tip drawing closer and closer to my entrance until he gently pushed inside me.

I gasped, and leaned back, stretching my arms out, giving him my body, knowing he'd satisfy me in the most incredible way.

He leaned over me, flicking his tongue over my nipples, sucking on them, worshiping them, all the while carefully working me up with slow, steady thrusts.

Heat pooled in my core and my breath picked up. A whisper of an orgasm shuddered through me and I gasped out a low throaty moan, drawing a masculine chuckle. But much to my disappointment, he fully withdrew, turning me so he could whisper in my ear.

"Float," he commanded, his hot breath teasing my sensitive skin.

I spread my arms and legs, the anticipation of what he planned next trembling through me, ratchetting up my desire. The water lapped around me, and for a moment I was alone, drifting peacefully in the waves, looking up at that amazing velvet sky with its silver moon and stars.

Then, he drew up under me, his chest pressed against my back, his tail swishing and sweeping down near my legs. His strong arms wrapped around me as I floated, his hands caressing up my belly to my breasts, a strange mix of relaxation and building tension heating my insides.

"This is incredible," I breathed.

"You're incredible," he replied, sliding his fingers back down my belly, through my curls, and into my folds.

My breath hitched and I released it on a moan to let him know how much I appreciated what he was doing. He nibbled on my ear, his fingers building up my need, the pace languid, as if we had all the time in the world.

And even though we didn't, even though my heart still broke over my missing bonds and I was terrified for my other guys, I let Del sweep me away with soft, warm sensation, just for a little while

Then his cock pressed between my butt cheeks and the idea of taking him there, of feeling the incredible pressure of him filling me, stole my breath completely.

"Oh yes," I gasped, shifting my hips and encouraging him to push inside me. "I need you."

"As my lady wishes," he replied, his voice thick with desire.

He swept his hands to my rear and spread me, his tip slowly pushing past the tight ring of muscle with a glorious lick of pain.

He entered me slowly, carefully, giving my body time to adjust to him. It felt like it took forever for him to burry himself completely within me, and I was gasping, trembling and more than ready for him by the time he was done.

Then he started to move, slowly at first, twisting my desire even tighter. His hands slid back around me, one coming up to cradle my breast while the other went down between my legs and rubbed circles on my clit.

I was already teetering on the brink from just having him enter me, and it didn't take long before another, more powerful orgasm washed over me. I cried out as my body shook, and he paused, his erection buried deep within me.

"More?" he whispered mischievously.

"Oh, gods, yes!" I huffed, my chest rising and falling as I sucked in great gulps of air.

He pulled halfway out and pushed back in again, his fingers still teasing my clit and pinching my nipple, sending aftershocks, rippling through me.

I sighed and moaned and trembled, loving every second of him filling me.

"You make the most incredible sounds," he gasped, his pace picking up as his desire started to overwhelm his control.

With a groan, he pushed two fingers inside me, matching his thrusts in my rear, his thumb grinding down on my clit, and his breath rushing past my cheek. His chest heaved against mine, his groans vibrating through me, and then he thrust hard, his cock swelling with his release.

He cried his pleasure with a long satisfying moan as his fingers slammed inside me, hitting my G-spot, and his hand on my breast clenched tighter. The force of him coming threw me over the edge again, sending another incredible orgasm crashing through me.

I let my bliss carry me away for a second, away from the heartbreaking emptiness inside me and away from my fears.

In that moment there was just Del and me, the warm, undulating water, and the sparkling stars above us.

We floated there, locked together for a long time, joined in the only way we could be joined in the moment, neither of us wanting to separate.

But eventually we had to. We had a mission to accomplish.

We returned to the camp with the others just as Poseia was saying goodbye to Janice. The young princess looked over at us and rolled her eyes.

"Young love," she said as if we were the ones younger than her, not the other way around. Then, more seriously, she whispered, "Take care of each other." Looking to Janice, she added. "All of you." She gave us all a lingering look, her pearl-blue eyes intense, then she walked into the waves and dove beneath the water.

"Are we ready?" I asked Janice. Del and I made our way into the light of the fire where our troops were, some quietly talking, others asleep, and I sat in Del's lap with his arms wrapped around me.

"You two go for a swim?" Janice asked with a wink. "Do a little breast stroke, maybe?"

I was sure I blushed all the way down to my afore-mentioned breasts.

Janice just smiled. "Yes, we're ready. Tomorrow, we're getting your guys back. It's all planned out."

That reassured me, though, as I fell asleep in Del's arms that night, I had the words of my high-school history teacher rolling through my head, "No plan survives contact with the enemy."

CHAPTER 9

ANNIE

"OH," I SAID A BIT DEFLATED. "THAT'S THE PLAN?"

Janice and I were walking down the beach toward the stones that would take us and our troops—boy it felt weird thinking that word—back to our world. She was telling me what she and Poseia had discussed the previous evening, and it seemed the plan, once we were back on our world, involved a bit of experimentation and exploration before we did anything.

Since everyone from this world would have some special ability in our world, we'd want to know what that was before we continued.

"That's the start of the plan," Janice said. "The hope is that among the thirty people we have here, there will be a few with abilities that might be useful for what we're planning. Our main liabilities at the moment are three-fold: first, we have to assume Hera is watching the portal so we won't have the element of surprise if we try to repeat what we did the last time. Second, we don't know where your friends are inside that building, or even if they are inside the building. And third, going in guns-blazing is a bad idea—as we've already figured out."

Yeah, I didn't want a repeat of the last time, but I'd hoped that between Janice and Poseia they'd have come up with an incredible plan, not 'take a moment and figure out what we've got.' Even if figuring out what the others could do was probably the best plan.

"Even if we don't count Hera, we're outnumbered and out gunned, so finding some other, more secret way in, even if we don't completely have the element of surprise would be preferable," Janice continued. "If some of those here have abilities which can help with either of the above problems that would significantly increase our chances of success, which means it's worth it to take a moment and find out what people can do. Besides we'll need clothes for most of them anyway. That's where your part of the plan comes in. As we're practicing abilities, and I'm figuring out whose abilities we can use, you'll be getting everyone clothes."

"I have no money."

"You've got a bank card."

"If I use it at an ATM, Hera will know where I am. Don't those things have cameras and stuff?"

"They do, which is why you'll take one of these new guys with you. If they use your card, it will look like you sold it or gave it away. They can empty your accounts and that would seem like the natural thing for some random person to do. They'll be the ones on camera, not you and Del. Once you have the cash, you can buy the clothes and get back to us, hopefully without being traced."

I nodded to that. It was actually rather smart.

"After that?" I asked.

"We'll see if anyone has any abilities to help us get in, then reevaluate from there. I've memorized the layout and blue-prints of Hera's tower and—"

"You did? Really? When?"

Janice smiled. "I've always had a good memory. I did it before we went in the first time."

"Oh."

"The only issue is, those were the official blue prints, she may have some hidden rooms we don't know about."

"Yeah, probably."

"Anyway, assuming we can get in without drawing too much attention, a small group of us will go and case the area tactically, then extract your friends and get the fuck out of there."

"I may be able to sense them, but I think I'd need to be fairly close," Del offered, as he approached from behind us.

"Oh?" Janice asked.

"Using my abilities with water, I can sense those I'm familiar with, their..." He frowned as if he was looking for the right words. "Their water-sense is different from others', unique. It's hard to explain."

"How close would you need to be?"

"I don't know," he replied. "Perhaps a hundred feet? With Annie the range was a lot greater, but I was also bonded to her. These are good friends, so I would hope I'd have a decent range, but I can't be certain offhand."

"That's good to know, but a bit uncertain. We'll see if one of the others can sense them from farther away, somehow. If not, you'll be our bloodhound once we're inside."

"Bloodhound?" Del asked.

"A type of dog with a good sense of smell," I explained. I'd seen dogs in this world so I knew that would make sense.

He nodded. "Bloodhound indeed."

"Any thoughts on the 'getting in secretly' part of the plan?" I asked.

Janice shrugged. "Let's hope one of them can help us." She indicated the group of twenty tritons and the mixed bag of ten others trailing behind us.

That reminded me. "How did things go with Naz yesterday? You seemed to be having a good time. I heard you laughing."

Janice blushed. I was fairly certain it was the first time I'd seen her do it. "He's charming and funny, yes."

"And?" I knew she'd slept alone last night.

She looked away, out over the sea. "He told me about... about our kind." She seemed to stumble over the word: 'our.' "It sounds nice, where he comes from, though, cold. It's high in the mountains. But his people spend hours on end soaring out over all these lands, high above, looking down." A heavy sigh escaped her. "A part of me... some part of me likes that idea, of soaring free, high in the sky, but..." She grimaced, and glanced back at me with a pained expression in her eyes. "That's not who I am... is it? I'm from our world. I'm an infectious disease specialist for the FBI. Aren't I?"

I could see the turmoil within her. She was going

through an existential crisis, not knowing who she really was.

"Once this is all over, you can come and go between worlds as you like. Well, I might have to help you, but we can work that out. Maybe if you spend some time here, you'll work out who and what you want to be."

"Thanks," she said with a half-smile. "I'd appreciate that."

"With everything you're doing—and have done—for me, it's the least I can do."

Her smile grew. "I can remember when I thought you were a goddess."

"You don't anymore?" I asked, curious what she now thought of me, but not upset that she no longer believed I was a goddess.

"Now I have wings. Everything has changed. I don't know what I think about anything."

That was fair.

I turned my attention ahead of us to the tall black rocks and the invisible portal back to my world.

"Once we're ready, I'll want to go through first and scout the other side. There's a decent chance Hera will be expecting us," Janice said, before hurrying away from us to go find her clothes where she'd hidden them.

Del and I found where we'd stashed ours and dressed amid odd looks from our new troop of followers.

I looked them over as I dressed. "Is there any way they can look more... human?" I asked Del. "Those minotaurs and the cyclops would really stand out in my world. Can they change, like you can?"

"They can," he replied, "but some may never have done it before. They'd have little need to."

Here was hoping changing to look like a human wasn't too difficult.

I pulled on my coat and turned to address the group. "Attention everyone. Where we're going, everyone looks like me. I've been told that you all can possibly do that as well? If so, please do so now. It will be much easier to blend in. We won't attract as much attention, which is the goal."

After a bit of murmuring and shuffling, there was a shift in the group. The minotaurs seemed to shrink a little—probably just from losing their horns—and looked fully human, though all three of them—including the woman—were bald. They instantly seemed awkward, stretching out their jaws and feeling their face, and slowly kicking out their legs.

The cyclops didn't shrink, but closed her one eye and then her face seemed to shimmer and she had two... in the right places. The *panai*'s legs shifted to look normal, his horns vanished, and his square eyes rounded. The various nymphs remained mostly unchanged. They couldn't adjust the mottled color of their skin—just like that disease-spreading naiad hadn't been able to be anything other than blue. The wings on the *nephelai* and on Naz disappeared, but their odd skin tone remained unchanged as well. Although unless anyone looked really closely, it would be good enough, Naz looked like some bronzed Greek god while the *nephelai* just looked extremely pale.

"Thank you!" I called out and went over to the stone where Janice was waiting with her gun ready.

"We have to assume there are forces on the other side, so I may be coming back quickly. Be ready," she said.

"Got it," I replied, pressing my hand against the stone.

She sucked in a deep breath then rushed through the portal.

My pulse pounded as I waited for her to return, fully expecting her to come running back with bullets following her.

But she didn't come back, which made me worried that she'd been captured right away.

I was about to go through myself, when she calmly stepped back through.

"It's clear," she said, but her expression was grim.

"Really?" That was a surprise. I was certain Hera knew about the portal and would be watching it.

Of course, maybe she thought I was so shattered at having lost my guys that I'd escaped with Del and wouldn't come back.

No. It had to be a trap... I just couldn't figure out how, and given that we had no way of knowing if we were being watched or not, we just had to continue with the plan until Hera attacked.

Or maybe things were actually going right for a change?

Yeah, I wasn't going to hold my breath on that.

And really, we had no choice. If we wanted to get to my world, we had to go through this portal.

It took a bit of time to get everyone across and by the time I went through last, the alley was crowded with thirty naked men and women who huddled together and shivered in the cold.

"I'll take them down this way, toward the dead-end of the alley—" Janice started before she was cut off.

"Annie Chambers?"

I spun toward the voice coming from the mouth of the alley.

Del jerked in front of me, blocking me from harm, and I peeked around him carefully.

There was only one man. He looked like one of Hera's goons, but he had his arms out and up.

"I have a message," he said.

I bet he did and I bet I wasn't going to like it.

I didn't trust any of this. Everything within me screamed that this was the trap I'd been expecting earlier.

Janice ran up to the man and frisked him, but didn't find a weapon… not that he'd need one if he was from the other world. He could have some kind of magic and we wouldn't know until he used it.

"The message is in my pocket," the man said, nodding to indicate the location. Janice got it out and he turned and left.

That was it?

No strike team repelling from the roofs around us, ready to capture or shoot us?

"That was not what I expected," Janice said as she came to me.

"Me, neither."

She handed over the envelope and I opened it carefully and drew out the small piece of monogramed paper inside.

.　.　.

ANNIE,

I HAVE YOUR BOYS, ALIVE AND VERY UNWELL. IF YOU WANT
to see them again, surrender yourself to me. I'll let them
go in exchange for you.

HERA

CHAPTER 10

ANNIE

I CRUMPLED UP THE PAPER, A MIX OF EMOTIONS CHURNING inside me.

A small, foolish part of me had hoped we'd be able to sneak back into my world and be able to free my guys, while the rest of me had expected an attack. Instead, I got confirmation that my guys were still alive—thank God!—and that Hera wanted to continue playing her sick game with me.

"Fuck." I knew she was a big cat, and cats liked to play with their prey, but fuck!

"This is… interesting," Janice said as she paced deeper into the alley then turned back toward us, her gaze turned inward in thought. "You must have something she needs. That's the only reason she didn't ambush us here. An ambush risks killing you and she clearly doesn't want to kill you. She needs you alive for some reason."

"Swell," I huffed. "I'd like to know why."

Janice shrugged. "I have no clue. We have to assume she's watching us somehow."

"Does that change the plan?" I asked.

"Yes. No. I don't know." She frowned and jerked around, heading deeper into the alley again. "Let me think." She reached the far end and came back. "I think the beginning part of the plan is the same. We still need money and clothes only... I don't think you should be out there with just a small guard around you. She might try to grab you. So you stay here and I'll go get the money and clothes."

"I'll go with you," Naz said stepping forward.

"All right. Here," Del replied and he stripped and handed the guy his clothes so he wasn't walking around Chicago naked.

It was a testament to how befuddled Janice must have been that she just nodded at him.

"We'll go and get the clothes. Del, you walk the rest of them through how to unlock their powers and see what we've got. Annie, stay in the middle of the group, hard to get at."

It sounded like a good plan to me, all things considered.

"Come on, fly-boy," Janice said, in control and seemingly forgetting her awkwardness around Naz, and they left the alley.

I turned to Del. "Time to find out what our crew can do," I said, even as my stomach churned with a new fear.

Hera could strike at any moment and the waiting was killing me. But what was worse, she wanted me alive, and I knew that wasn't a good thing.

We spent the next couple of hours trying to figure out what powers everyone had.

There was a wide array of abilities, from the useful, to the odd and weird. One of the *epimelidai* could turn himself into living fire! That discovery caused a whole bunch of burns in the tight alley, which I then had to heal. The female minotaur could read people's thoughts and the *nephelai* had powers of wind, like Hera, so maybe he could counter her attacks? Though I suspected Hera would be stronger than someone who'd only just discovered their powers.

Most of the powers the tritons had weren't that useful. One had a foul stench, and we were forced to make the poor guy stand at the far end of the alley. Another had an extendable and prehensile tongue, which might be useful in other circumstances, but not for combat, and a third guy began producing oily ink from his pores. The rest of the tritons simply didn't know what, if any powers, they had. Either they were too subtle to see, or not easily manifested.

The cyclops also couldn't seem to figure out what she could do, though she was strong to begin with. Similarly, one of the male minotaurs didn't know what he could do, while the other minotaur seemed to be able to sense people's emotions. He didn't seem impressed by this.

There were, however, a few useful abilities. The second *epimelidai* could blend in with any background, camouflaging himself, while the *panai* could shapeshift into anything—which might be good for scouting.

The *oreadai* could jump from place to place in an instant, and take others with him, which could get us into Hera's building quickly and undetected, and I knew he'd be coming with us for sure.

The other useful power came from one of the tritons who could seemingly sense through solid objects. He was confused as to exactly how it worked, but I realized it might allow us to 'see' what was on the other side of doors before we went through. He couldn't do it at any extreme range, but we'd still be bringing him along.

By the time Janice returned, I had a good idea of who'd make up our smaller strike-rescue team. Aside from myself and Del—and probably Janice and potentially Naz—we'd take the mind-reading minotaur, the teleporting *oreadai*, the sense-through-things triton, and the shape-shifting *panai*. The rest would be responsible for creating a distraction outside of Hera's tower in hopes of drawing some of her forces outside.

I wasn't concerned about learning the names of everyone here, that would be too much at once, but I did try to learn the names of the few who were going with us. Yelling, 'hey *oreadai*' in the middle of a fight might work, but it would be more polite to actually use his name.

The minotaur woman was Khyrys, the *oreadai* was Dorios, the *panai*, who seemed to be playing with how many different shapes he could take, went by Rhoumin or Rhou, and the triton was Ladon.

When Janice did return, it was with two shopping carts nearly overflowing with clothes, and a very ill-looking Naz.

"Please send him back to his world," Janice said, her voice tight with concern.

"What happened?" I asked as I activated the portal.

Janice helped the man stagger through. He could

barely walk and he clutched his head as if it hurt. He seemed about to retch, or collapse, or both.

She returned through the portal a moment later, her expression grim.

"I don't know what hit him. It seems like this world was just... too much for him," she said. "Before he got too bad, he said he could hear and smell things. I think his senses went nuts or something. Eventually he got a headache and could barely walk. I hurried back here as quick as I could. Unfortunately, that means the clothes selection is a bit slipshod. I was just grabbing stuff off racks. We'll see if we have enough and who fits what, and how good it looks."

Luckily the most of what Janice had gotten was bulky cold weather gear, which covered most of the armor the men wore. In the end, most of our force had decent clothes, if looking a bit haphazard. A few didn't have pants, so we gave them the longest coats, while a few others looked like they were about to head to the north pole in all their bulkiness, but it would work. Rhou, the shape-shifter, didn't need clothes, he could seemingly create them when he shifted, which meant one of the tritons trying not to shiver, did get pants.

Then we were ready. A small force of the tritons would stay and guard the alley, while the rest of us piled into a series of cabs and made our way downtown. And I could only pray that this would work. If not, we'd be dead... or become Hera's prisoners, likely wishing we were dead.

CHAPTER 11

My heart pounded as I materialized in a utility room in Hera's building. For a moment, I hadn't been anywhere, lost in darkness, feeling like I was in a million places at once, yet still feeling Del's warm hand holding mine.

The *panai*, Rhou, fell to his knees and lost his breakfast. Ladon, the triton, staggered, but didn't fall, though he took a long moment to come back to himself, while Del swayed, blinking, but remained standing.

"That was..." Janice flashed a hint of a smile, seeming to have coped the best out of all of us. "That was fun!"

She had a strange idea of fun.

As the rest of us took a moment, Janice inspected the room. We were in a small space packed with shelves with cleaning supplies and boxes, on a sub-level of the building.

"Rhou, feel up for some scouting?" Janice asked.

The *panai*, though he didn't seem fully recovered

from Dorios's teleportation magic yet, nodded. "Of course, Miss Janice."

"Take the form of a mouse and scout through the vents. See if you can find an *erinai*, a stone titan, and a satyr," she said, the other world's terminology easily rolling off her tongue.

Rhou nodded and an instant later was scurrying off as a mouse toward a grate at the base of one of the walls.

Now we had to sit tight and wait, just like the rest of our force outside. The plan was for them to hide for a couple hours before they attacked, drawing out the guards in the building. We could only hope those few hours would be enough time for Rhou to figure out where everyone was, return, and for us to come up with a plan.

No one said anything while we waited, and while I considered sitting, I didn't want to get caught on my ass if anyone found us. And from the way no one else sat, I suspected they thought the same thing.

My pulse pounded, my blood rushing in my ears, and my stomach churned. Without a doubt Hera was waiting for us. I could only hope that the magical abilities the others had gained would give us enough of an advantage to help Rion, Aethan, and Keph escape.

That was the main goal. As much as I wanted to bring Hera down for good, I had to get my guys out of there first.

I turned to Del, whose expression was hard, the muscles in his jaw flexed.

"Can you sense Rion and the others?" I asked, hoping

he'd be able to feel the unique 'water-sense' of the other three men.

Del closed his eyes and after a long moment shook his head. "There's too much steel and stone around. I can't sense far. All I know is they're not close."

I'd assumed that much already. If Hera wasn't keeping them in the basement, it made sense for her to keep them in her apartment on the top floor.

But man, I wanted to free them now. Now now now.

Frustration twisted in my stomach as I fought to ignore the ache of my missing bonds.

"We'll find them," he said, caressing small circles on my back as if he could sense my frustration.

"I know," I murmured back while a part of me whispered, *but in what condition?*

Del shifted closer, as if knowing I needed more than a back rub, and wrapped his arms around me. "We *will* find them," he murmured. "We—"

But swift-marching, booted footfalls sounded in the corridor beyond our room cut him off and we all went quiet, tensing as the footfalls stopped just outside our door.

CHAPTER 12

ANNIE

CRAP. CRAP CRAP CRAP. SOMEONE WAS IN THE HALL RIGHT outside the door.

Janice shot a hard glance at Khyrys, telling her to read the mind of whoever was out there, while the others clenched their hands, preparing for a fight, and I held my breath, praying we wouldn't get caught.

"It's me, Rhou," came a deep and resonant voice from outside, and Khyrys nodded her confirmation.

I frowned. It certainly didn't sound like the *panai*, but then, if he was in another form, it wouldn't.

The door cracked open and a tall man clad in black body armor and a helmet entered, his hands up as if he feared we'd pounce on him even though we had a mind reader in our group. Then he carefully shut the door behind him and melted back into Rhou's short, slight form.

I let out a heavy breath I hadn't known I'd been holding. "What did you find?"

"I found the men we're looking for," he said, his

expression grim. "But they're not in a good way. They'll probably need our help getting out, and one of them is with a woman on the top floor. I'm assuming that's Hera?"

"Fuck," I hissed, my heartrate rising. "Of course, she'd told me to come, so she'd want at least one of the guys with her for insurance."

"But why not all three?" Janice asked.

"If they're all in one spot, they'd be easier to rescue," Del suggested.

Janice nodded at that. "True."

"Where are the other two?" I asked Rhou.

His expression grew even darker. "They're in rooms a couple floors below where Hera is. "They..." he trailed off and frowned.

What? They... what?

"Are they alive?"

Please be alive.

"They are, but they've been badly hurt."

I turned to Dorios. "Can you teleport us to them?"

Dorios turned to Janice. "Draw me a map so I can concentrate on it, just like how we got here."

"What floor were they on?" Janice asked Rhou.

"Ah... I don't know the number, sorry."

Janice paced for a moment in the small cramped space, the others leaning back against the shelves to make room for her. "You said a couple floors below Hera's suite? Exactly two floors?"

Rhou blinked a bit, then closed his eyes, perhaps trying to remember and retrace his steps. "Ah... well, yes and no. Two floors below where Hera was, there was a door. It led to a stairway, which was the only access to a floor below that. As far as I could tell, there was no other way to get to that third floor down, and that's where the men were being held."

"A secret floor in the building?" Janice paused her movement and her eyes scanned back and forth as if she was looking at something, except she didn't seem to be seeing anything around her. "Yeah, that's not on the blue prints. Damn. I'm not sure I'll be able to draw anything accurate."

She returned to pacing, muttering to herself. I watched her, silently praying she'd be able to figure this out.

"Rhou..." Janice said, slowly.

"Yes?" He leaned closer, his gaze locked on her. There was something in his eyes, something—

A faint smile curled my lips despite the grim news. He was looking at Janice the same way my guys looked at me. He was infatuated with her. And if we got out of this alive, I was going to make sure those two had, in the very least, a conversation and got to know each other.

"Dorios..." Janice said.

The young man perked up, waiting for his instructions.

Janice frowned, then turned to Khyrys, the minotaur with the ability to read minds. "Could you take a picture from someone's mind and share it with someone else?"

The minotaur woman, no longer looking like a minotaur at all, raised a single brow. "I don't know. I can read minds, but putting something into another's mind..."

"Just try," Janice said. "Try to speak into my mind or project some image or thought."

Silence sank over the room as the two women stared intently at each other. It seemed to take forever before both sets of eyes widened.

"Yes!" Janice gasped. "Great! Now Rhou, bring to mind where you found the three guys and share those thoughts with Khyrys."

I began to sense where this was going. If Dorios could be given Rhou's thoughts as to where the guys were, perhaps he could teleport directly to them.

Within a few minutes, the location images had been conveyed to Dorios and then the *oreadai* started talking with Rhou about how high the building was to try to get a sense for the location in space.

Janice came to me as the other two worked through this.

"Here's what I'm thinking," she said. "Dorios drops us off in a secluded corner of Hera's suites. Then he jumps in and frees your two guys on the lower levels, taking them to the alley, where they'll hopefully be safe until we can meet up with them."

I nodded. As much as I wanted to see them right away, it was better to get them out of danger first. Once everyone was safe, then I'd have a chance to reunite with them... as bittersweet as that might be with our missing bonds.

"Meanwhile," Janice continued, "we make our way to Hera, and wait for Dorios to return. Once he's back, we'll create a distraction, so he can jump in to free the last one. Hera will probably know the instant he's in the room with her, given her advanced senses. So, we make like we're going to hand you over, which will hopefully be enough of a distraction for Dorios to get in an out. There will be even more of a distraction if we time this to happen while our force outside is attacking." She checked her watch. "In about a half hour."

My heart pounded so hard I thought it would tear out of my chest. I didn't want to wait. I couldn't stand another minute of doing nothing. I needed to see them and heal them and—

I shoved those thoughts as deep down as I could. I couldn't let them distract me.

This was the best plan we were going to get given the circumstances and I needed to keep my head and follow it, no matter what my heart wanted.

"Sounds good," I forced out and Janice turned to confirm the plan with the others.

Del drew close again and wrapped his arms around me. "How are you doing?"

"Horrible," I confided. "I can't get my nerves straight. I'm so worried about the guys and about these folks and those outside. I don't want anyone to get hurt, but..." I was talking a mile a minute, shaking with urgency and fear.

He tightened his embrace. "We're almost there."

I nodded into his chest, but secretly there was a much deeper worry in my heart. With luck—gods, please give us luck—we'd have my guys all free soon, but my bond with them was still broken. Del and I had been very intimate a couple of times now and it hadn't reformed, and I was beginning to think that Hera had taken that away from me permanently. If so...

No. I didn't want to contemplate that, either.

I'd die without my guys. And just having them around, would be good enough. It had to be. Except I feared I'd still feel hollow without their bonds even if they were close. And if I couldn't get over that, how would that effect our relationship?

I tried to push those thoughts aside with the others as time inched closer to the moment when the rest of our team would create their distraction.

Then all of a sudden Janice looked up. "Ready?" she asked. "It's time."

I nodded with the rest, but in my heart—my desperate, thundering heart—I was terrified and not ready at all.

CHAPTER 13

DELPHON

Dorios whisked us from the utility room to a hallway then vanished again. The hall was short with a door at one end with a symbol that looked like stairs, and at the other end, the hall turned right and kept going.

"Where are we?" Annie asked in a whisper.

"One of the only unguarded places close to Hera," Janice whispered back. "We're one floor below her and next to the stairs." She pointed to the door with the stairs symbol then turned to Ladon who could see through walls. "How many people are around?"

He put a hand against the closest wall and closed his eyes. "Two just beyond that door to the stairs. Another two directly above them and a group of four down that hallway." He pointed to the open end of the hall then bent his finger to indicate they were down a little.

I stared at him. I knew he could *see through* things. I just hadn't realized he didn't need to be looking in that direction to do so.

"They must be at the elevators," Janice whispered as if

she thought I was confused about the direction he'd been pointing. Which I hadn't been, but now I was. I had no idea what an elevator was.

"There are a few more upstairs," Ladon reported.

"Del," Annie said turning to me. "You're up."

I clenched my jaw and gave her a tight nod. I wasn't happy about what was to come next. I didn't want to use my powers to kill people, but things were dire and I was the only one in our group with a magic that could be used offensively.

I crept to the door to the stairs. There was a small vertical window in it and I peeked through it. I could see both men on the other side of the door, wearing that same black armor and helmet as the rest of Hera's men, and I reached out with my water abilities.

The body was mostly water and I could feel everyone around me, but I focused on the two on the other side of the door and began pulling the water out of them.

I heard the gasps and groans from both of them as they must have suddenly felt... well I had no clue what that would feel like, but I guessed it was painful, probably very uncomfortable at the least.

Then both men fell with a heavy thud and I felt their bodies curling in on themselves as they lost more and more water. I halted before—what I hoped—was a fatal stage, then wrenched open the door and rushed inside, ready to finish them off in case I'd failed to incapacitate them.

But they weren't in any condition to attack. They lay at my feet, looking gaunt and surprised, squirming and unable to speak, the sight making my stomach churn. Gods, they looked horrible. And I'd done that to them.

"Quickly," I hissed, not wanting to kill men who were just doing their jobs like the soldiers who'd come with me from Galniosia. "They'll recover in time, but they're out for now." Though, even as I finished saying this, I heard footsteps coming down the stairs from above.

The guards on the landing above us must have heard something.

I closed my eyes and reached out again.

This time I felt men both above and below us. There was one figure descending from above and another staying up on the landing, as well as two on the floor below us, one of them tentatively coming up a few stairs.

I reached out to all of them and pulled on their water.

In a moment, they were all writhing and incapacitated like the two before me.

Then something *popped* and agony screamed through my leg. I fell to the ground, hands clamped around my injury and forced myself to look up the stairs for whoever had attacked me. One of the guards had managed to reach the landing at the turn in the stairs just above me, and had used his *gun*. Though he only got off one shot and was now writhing and gasping on the floor, severely dehydrated.

Annie knelt next to me. "Let me see."

I started to peel my hand away, but blood, which had been oozing from my fingers, now gushed over my hand and down my leg, and I pressed back down on the wound.

Annie slapped her hands over top of mine and the

blood flow eased enough for me to remove my hand. A moment later the small metal projectile was pushed out of the wound by Annie's healing magic and the pain faded.

"Thank you," I murmured.

"Let's go," Janice hissed. "They're using silencers so hopefully no one heard that, but I don't want to wait around to find out."

We hurried up the stairs, then waited at the door.

Time crept by before Dorios appeared with us as planned.

"The other two are safe," he said, and a pressure in my chest eased a bit.

Thank the gods! At least two of my friends were safe. Now there was only one left in dire trouble. And while I still feared what Hera could do, I had hope Janice's plan would work.

We hurried through the next doorway, keeping quiet, and I disabled the four guards down the hall, who stood in front of two odd-looking metal doors. Perhaps these were the *elevators* Janice had mentioned.

Then, just outside of Hera's rooms, we paused and Ladon and I felt for people.

"Four just inside," Ladon reported. "Another four in a room beyond, one on their knees. About a dozen more not too far away in this complex of rooms."

I could only feel the four nearby.

"Fuck," Annie hissed. "That's a lot."

"Let's do this quickly," Janice said. "Del?"

My turn again. I pulled water from the four on the other side of the door where we waited, then all of us, except for Dorios, charged in. He remained hidden, keeping one door open just a little to peer through since he needed to see where he was jumping to and there was a chance whoever was being held there had been moved since Rhou had last been there.

The room beyond was a large foyer area with a few chairs and a flagrant display of wealth: lavish tapestries, large pieces of art, and pedestals with vases or glass cases displaying valuables. It was meant to impress, and it did.

"Annie, so nice of you to join us!" Hera proclaimed. She stood holding one of Rion's wings to keep him upright—the *erinai* only seemed to have one—with a small *gun* to the back of his head. Two more men in armor stood behind her.

"Rion!" Annie shouted, her voice cracking with pain and concern. He looked horrible with cuts and bruises all over his naked body. He was barely conscious, held upright on his knees only by Hera's grip.

"My security tells me you've already freed your two other friends. I don't know how, but trust that this one will not—"

It happened so quickly we were all stunned. Dorios jumped in, grabbed Rion while prying Hera's hand off his wing, and teleported away.

My thoughts stuttered.

They were gone.

And *I* been expecting it.

Hera looked stunned, blinking at her now empty hand as if she couldn't figure out what had happened. "What—?"

She raised her *gun* as did the two men behind her, but

the rest of us had joined hands by then. A spray of bullets roared from their weapons as Dorios popped in behind us and yanked us back to the alley. I was sure I'd been staring at one of those projectiles only inches away when we'd left.

My heart was racing as I staggered back. My shoulder blades hit the cold brick wall and I sagged to the ground.

"We did it?" Annie asked, her tone hesitant as if she didn't believe it.

And gods, it had happened so fast, I still wasn't sure we'd actually done it.

"Almost. We need to get the others away from Hera's tower now!" Janice said and Dorios was gone again.

Dorios brought the others back in small groups, but it quickly became apparent that their assault hadn't gone well. Far too many were wounded, dying, or dead and with Annie the only one able to heal and open the portal, she decided to save those who were critically injured instead of opening the portal, fearing they wouldn't last long enough to get to our world.

She helped everyone she could, jumping from one person to the next, as Dorios brought in group after group. She even managed to heal Aethan, Rion, and Keph, who'd also been severely injured, but not enough for them to regain consciousness.

She was staggering toward one of my fellow tritons, looking exhausted and barely able to stay upright when the sound of cars roared nearby.

Both Annie and Janice's gazes jumped to the mouth of the alley, and Annie jerked toward the wall where the portal lay.

"Back through the portal now!" she said.

I grabbed Rion, while one of the minotaurs lifted Aethan, and the two other minotaurs, the cyclops, and three tritons picked up Keph.

We staggered through and I handed Rion off to two other tritons then stood by the rocks, watching everyone else run through, and waited for Annie.

My heart pounded. I couldn't see or hear anything. Nothing from her side could be seen through the portal to our side and I didn't want to get in the way of those escaping to go check on her.

I hurriedly counted who'd already come through and who was left.

The last triton rushed passed me and then Annie staggered through, bleeding from several wounds. Her gaze lifted as if she was trying to look at me before her eyes rolled back and she collapsed onto the sand, unconscious.

CHAPTER 14

AETHAN

I SCREAMED, JERKING UPRIGHT IN A COLD SWEAT, desperately looking around, but not able to focus on anything. Then my vision started to clear and I saw sand. A vast, warm stretch of sand with a large group of people nearby.

I was on a beach.

Oh thank all the gods!

I was safe... unless I wasn't.

My pulse leaped, pounding in my chest. I had to be dreaming. This had to be a vision my mind made up so I could escape the pain and horror.

Except if this was a dream, why were there so many people I didn't know wandering around.

"Aethan?" a familiar voice called out, and I dragged my gaze behind me as Del rushed over to me.

"You're awake. Good," he said, kneeling beside me.

"Am I?" I asked, my pulse trying to return to normal even though I still wasn't sure if I was dreaming or not.

Del frowned. "Are you what?"

"Awake."

He stared at me as if he had no idea what to say then grabbed me, wrapping his strong arms around me in a brotherly embrace.

"Aethan, you're safe," he assured me. "We got you out. No more danger. Annie healed you and we're in our world now."

More of my fear bled away, and I almost completely believed him. All that remained was a tiny voice of self-preservation that wouldn't allow me to completely hope and be happy just yet. I needed more proof.

I hugged Del back, then we released each other and I stood, my body complaining at the movement. But just being able to stand was astounding... which didn't completely add to Del's assurance that I wasn't dreaming.

Hera had been thorough in her torture.

A shudder swept through me and I tried to shove back the memory. I didn't want to recall any of it. She'd cut the tendons in my legs and done something to my hoofed feet, but there was no indication that I'd been hurt. My body was whole, if sore and aching.

Taking a tentative step, I easily found my balance even if the rest of me, my mind and emotions were unsteady. I'd wanted to die and I'd been terrified Annie had died. I still was terrified, even if Del had just said she'd healed me. There was an aching hollowness in my chest where she was supposed to be, and I was afraid it meant she was dead. My mate, my goddess was dead.

"She really did a number on you guys," Del said, his voice soft and grim.

I couldn't answer, not yet, maybe not ever. That would

require remembering and I didn't want to remember. Instead, I gave a tight nod, unable to fully make eye contact and started shuffling around, trying to work out the pain in my body.

Except that made me think of being strapped to Hera's table and—

"How are the others?" I forced out, trying to change the conversation in my mind, but unable to really think of anything else.

"You're the first awake," Del replied, watching me walk in slow, unsteady circles.

I glanced around and saw Keph and Rion laying not far away… and Annie.

My pulse lurched. She lay beside them, still in her other world clothes, the fabric covered in blood even though her complexion looked fine, like there wasn't anything wrong with her. But something had to be wrong because I couldn't feel our bond.

"Oh gods, Annie," I gasped, jerking toward her and losing my balance.

Del caught me. "She'll be okay. She was hurt holding the portal open when we returned, but she's healing herself even though she's unconscious. She looks a lot better now than she did before. I'm sure she'll be awake shortly."

I leaned in his grip, unable to go anywhere else but to her side and Del helped me, as if he knew I had to go to her.

"I can't feel her anymore," I said, my voice tight with grief as Del helped me sag to the sand beside her. "Something happened just before she got thrown out the window. I thought she'd died."

"Janice, that FBI woman, caught her. Turns out she was a hidden *aurai* all along, and she sprouted wings and saved them both."

"Hidden *aurai*?" I asked confused. What was that supposed to mean?

"She's from their world, but I'm guessing a long time ago her ancestors got together with some *aurai*. It was in her blood, but dormant until a crisis brought it out. That's my guess. She was quite shocked about it for a while there."

"Hunh."

I had no idea what to say to that. I wanted to thank the gods that Annie was alive, but remembered what Hera had done to me and thought better of it. Better to just stick to cursing them.

I brushed a lock of soft red hair away from Annie's cheek, the ache of her absence inside me swelling as I looked at her, and cupped her cheek. She didn't stir, and if I didn't look at her damaged body, I could almost think she was just asleep.

"Why can't I feel her?" I might have been able to endure so much more if I'd felt my bond with Annie, but that had vanished, leaving a gaping wound in my soul.

"Hera did something to Annie which removed her bonds with us." Del sighed. "We've tried to get it back, but nothing has worked so far."

That didn't sound good at all.

A few feet away someone grunted, then grunted

again, and Keph slowly sat up, his hands pressed against his temples as if his head hurt.

"Where...?" His gaze darted around and landed on us and Annie. "Annie?"

"She'll be fine," Del reassured, except I could hear the tension in his voice. She might be physically fine, but her soul was broken like ours was, her bonds missing. "How are you doing?"

Keph gave another heavy grunt. "Hera tried really hard to hurt me. It took a lot and tired her out. I don't think I was much fun." He rolled to his hands and knees, then slowly climbed to his feet, not looking as effected as I was. "What happened to Annie?"

"She got hurt when we left the other world. She's healing. She'll be fine," Del insisted.

Keph sat heavily on the other side of her and nodded. "Good." He looked over at us. "You two? How are you?"

Del glanced at me and I grimaced.

"I..." I didn't want to say how I felt. I was weak and terrified. "I'll be well. Eventually."

Del nodded at that. "I wasn't taken. I'm well enough." He looked around at the others on the beach not too far away. "But I'll be paying back my mother for the rest of my life," he murmured.

I didn't understand what that meant and was about to ask when Keph spoke up first.

He pressed his large hand over his heart and frowned. "What happened to our bond?"

Del explained it to Keph, and even hearing it for a second time, it still felt wrong. It was even worse to see

Keph's expression fall, his heartbreak clear on his face, the same heartbreak I felt.

"It was rough being separated from her," he rumbled.

"Yeah," I agreed.

Del swallowed, the muscles in his jaw flexing. "I know."

We didn't say much after that, just watched Annie, or the others on the beach, or the distant waves.

After a while of silence, Keph finally drew in a deep breath and squared his massive shoulders. "What do we do now?"

I didn't know about the other two, but I'd been waiting for Rion or Annie to wake up and hadn't thought much beyond that.

"I think we rest and heal and..." Del shrugged. "I don't know." He opened his mouth as if to continue then shook his head. "I don't know. Hera seems unstoppable." The fight seemed to have gone out of him. He just kept shaking his head. "I'm just glad we have all of you back."

"How did you do that anyway?" I asked. "I was only half aware of what was going on. I was there then... not."

Del glanced around then pointed at an *oreadai* talking with a triton and a female minotaur. "See that *oreadai* over there?"

I nodded.

"We all have powers in the other world. We found that he could jump from place to place. Annie called it *teleporting*. That's how we got you out. Another fellow... Ah... Rhou—that *panai* over there." He pointed at another man standing a few feet away from the first one. "He can change shapes and did some scouting around to find you. Then the *oreadai* pulled you out. You two were easy, Rion... was with *her*. That took precise timing and we almost all died."

There was something he wasn't saying, but I wasn't going to push him on it and Annie let out a long, drawn-out groaning breath, stopping whatever else he might have said.

"Fuck me," she groaned as we all turned to her. "That hurt."

"What happened?" Del asked.

She raised her arm to shield her eyes from the late day sun, her gaze jumping from him to me then to Keph, a warm, sad smile pulling at her lips. "Soldiers arrived as the last of us were going through. I was shot several times as I ducked into the portal. I can safely say I don't want to be shot ever again."

She half rose, sitting propped up on one arm and looked down at herself. "I can still feel it even though the wounds seem to be gone." She sat up fully, rolling her shoulders and moving around a bit, flinching with some movement. "It may take a bit to get rid of that remembered pain, I think."

"But you're alive." I wrapped my arms around her, pulling her to my chest in a tight embrace, never wanting to let her go. "I'm so glad you're alive."

She weakly returned my hug as if even though she was awake she was still exhausted. "I missed you, too. All of you. Is Rion...?"

"Not up yet," Keph rumbled looking back over at the still prone form of our last brother.

She sighed heavily. "He..." She shuddered and something sad and angry darkened her expression. "Gods."

I wasn't certain I wanted to know what was going through her mind. Annie had healed me, so she'd known what Hera had done to me, and I had a feeling what Hera had done to Rion had been worse.

"I... I need to walk." She extracted herself from my reluctant-to-let-her-go embrace and stood. I was up next to her in a flash as Keph rose as well.

"No," she said, seeing all of us ready to go with her. "I can't... not everyone, not right now." She pressed her hand to her chest, as if she too felt the emptiness of our missing bond—

Gods, she was missing all four of us.

If missing just her was bad, missing all four of us had to be horrible.

"You shouldn't be alone," Del insisted, a strange fear in his eyes that I'd never seen before. "You're still weak. If something happened..."

She sighed. "You're right. Just one of you then," she offered.

We all looked at each other. The desperation I felt to stay close to her must have shown in my eyes, because the other two nodded at me, agreeing I should be the one to go with her.

Thank the gods.

Annie stripped away her bloody clothes and began a brisk walk toward the hills, away from the beach, as if she wanted to get away from everyone. I got the feeling she wanted to be completely alone but had let me come along as a compromise, so I kept my mouth shut. And even if she had wanted to talk, I wasn't sure what I could say. I didn't want to bring up what had happened or the empty ache inside me. Yeah, perhaps not talking was best right now.

Once we were well away from the beach she finally slowed. She gave a half-hearted chuckle, which didn't last and didn't seem to particularly reflect her dour mood. "You're not as fast here."

I gave a similar short, breathy laugh. "No, I'm not. If I were in horse-form I'd be much faster."

She turned to me then, one brow raised. "I don't think I've ever seen you in horse form. Would you mind showing me? Can you talk in horse form?"

I shifted for her. It was easy enough. I didn't spend much time as a horse, but there was something about the more powerful form which made me feel more confident, less like an empty, bondless failure. "Yes, I can still talk."

"You sound a little funny though," she giggled and drew up next to me, running a hand over my long neck and flank. She slowly came to embrace me, her hands around the base of my neck, and I rested my large head lightly on her back, not able to do much else.

We stayed that way for a long time, just touching each other before she started softly weeping.

"Annie?" I murmured.

She sniffled. "I'll be okay." She didn't sound like she would be.

"What do you need?"

"Can you... stay like this for a while?"

I wasn't sure why. "Of course."

Silence stretched out again as we simply stood there,

her arms wrapped around me.

Finally, she drew in a shuddering breath and released me. "Can I..." She came around so I could see her more easily, sliding both of her hands along my snout. She had an odd look. "Can I ride you?"

I whinnied—which was my horse version of a laugh. "Of course."

Just those two small words and her eyes lit up. It made my heart sing that I was the one to bring her such joy with something so simple.

Carefully, I knelt so she could straddle me, and once her legs were clenched tight to my sides and her hands digging into my mane, I rose.

"Is this okay? Am I hurting you?" she asked.

A little. Her grip in my mane was a little too tight, but I wasn't going to complain. "No."

I began to walk slowly.

"Oh!" she said and her legs squeezed tighter, as did her hands in my mane. I tried to ignore the pain. My flanks could take it, but my mane felt like it was going to be torn out.

"Are you stable?" I asked. Turning my head to look back. She seemed to be faring well enough. She looked like a queen, proud and tall, riding bareback. I was momentarily distracted by the movement of her breasts as I walked, but I turned away eventually.

"Faster?" she said, and I eased into a slow trot.

Again, she tightened her hold on me.

"I want to feel you run, feel your power. I want to feel free and unburdened, to forget everything!"

I picked up the pace slowly, from a fast trot to a

canter. I felt her duck lower, pressing herself against my back, one hand reaching around my neck.

"Yes!" she whooped, close to my ear, her voice filled with joy.

I slipped into a full gallop for a moment before slowing again to check on her. There was a wildness in her eyes as if she was determined to force away the bad memories and feelings and just be free.

"More," she whispered, and I ran.

Annie whooped and shouted, wordless cries of joy and grief and release.

I was a bit lathered by the time I stopped, and Annie slid off my back quickly, stumbling, and leaning against me to keep her balance.

"Oh! My legs are sore," she laughed, but her voice was edged with something else, something desperate.

I glanced back at her, her hair was windswept and wild, her complexion flush with the exertion of riding.

"Switch back," she said, the desperation thickening. "I need you."

I didn't need to be told twice. I was in my satyr form again in an instant. Annie had her body up against mine, and captured my mouth with hers. I responded in kind, already well aroused and ready from having her ride me in my horse form.

The wild, needy kiss lasted only a moment before she urged me to the ground and straddled me yet again, this time in a way I much preferred. Grabbing my erection—with perhaps a bit too much force—she positioned it and lowered herself onto it with an exhalation of breath through her bared teeth.

Stones dug into my back, but I didn't care. The pain was a small price to pay for this pleasure, a pleasure she seemed to desperately need.

I reached up to hold her breasts, cupping and caressing, feeling their weight, and her already aroused nipples.

She tossed her head back, arms up, reaching skyward, as her hips ground and rocked against me. It was raw and desperate sex, no emotion other than a raging need. She was gasping and moaning, her body tensing as she pleasured herself on my cock.

"Harder," she moaned, and since she was already in control and grinding hard with her hips, I took her words to mean the work with my hands. I tightened my grip on her breasts, grasping and kneading the soft skin a she pressed more of her weight down upon me. "Yes!"

A hiss of breath escaped her lips and with eyes full of burning lust and desperation and heartache she looked down at me, capturing my soul. Gods, she was almost scary in her intensity, except I understood it, understood she was trying to fill the emptiness of our missing bond the only way she knew how.

I could tell she was nearing her peak, her motions quickening, frenzied, and I could feel my own release build.

"Come with me," she said, a demand, as her breath caught and her body stiffened. Her hips rocked one last time, forceful and jerking and I did as she commanded. I felt her muscles tighten around my cock, squeezing so hard I could feel her pulse, and my release crashed over me.

"Yes!" she gasped. "Yes."

Tears misted her eyes and she slowly sagged forward and lay on top of me. I wrapped my arms around her, her head on my chest tucked under my chin, and she cried again. This time her tears turned to heavy gaping, heartrending sobs as she cried out her heartache.

I didn't know what to do. There wasn't anything I could do. Del had said they'd tried to fix their broken bond and couldn't. Our bond hadn't reformed either with our kiss or during sex and I didn't know if I would ever be able to fix it.

I held her close, murmuring soothing noises. This wasn't the reaction a man hoped for after sex, but I knew it wasn't me. I'd given her something she'd desperately needed and now, only now, could she allow herself to release what had been pent up within her.

"I'm going to need to move soon," I whispered. "There's a rock digging into my butt and given your... intensity, I think I might be bleeding."

Her now quiet sobs shifted to a jerking, awkward laughter.

"I'll heal that for you," she said through her sniffles. Lifting herself up, her sunrise pale-red hair a curtain around us as her face hovered over mine.

"Thank you," she whispered, then lowered herself to kiss me lightly. As she withdrew, she said, "Sorry. I was a little... aggressive. My knees and thighs are killing me."

I laughed a little with her, and she smiled, the look in her stunning golden eyes filled with love and warmth and gratitude and sadness.

CHAPTER 15

HYPERION

I woke with a start, my heart pounding for a second before grief swept through me. I'd lost my wing. I'd lost Annie. I'd—

My thoughts stuttered. I wasn't strapped to Hera's table, I wasn't in pain, and I wasn't on my stomach. Right. I vaguely recalled being freed and whisked away from that horrible place.

I lay on my back, a warm breeze sweeping over my naked skin, staring up at a brilliant blue sky that called to me, begged me to take flight.

Except I couldn't. Hera had cut off my wing and if Annie was dead than an injury like that couldn't be fixed. I was flightless and that, added to the emptiness in my soul where Annie should have been, threatened to consume me. I couldn't push past the grief. And usually when my thoughts were too heavy, I'd fly. There was something about soaring high above everything that helped to clear my mind.

I knew I should have been happy. I was back on my own world and...

Back... on my own world?

But the only one who could open the portal was... Annie.

She had to be alive!

I looked around, but couldn't see her. Del and Keph spoke quietly nearby, but I couldn't see Annie or Aethan. Still... if I was here then...

I jerked up and pushed my wings out of my body. Both wings.

My pulse froze.

I had both of my wings. Somehow, by some miracle, I could still fly.

No.

Not a miracle... because of Annie.

She'd saved me twice. Somehow freeing me from Hera and then giving me back my wings, and yet my soul was still shattered at what had happened, at how helpless I'd been. I, a trained warrior, had been useless. I hadn't been able to stop Hera, hadn't been able to protect my friends, or my mate. And even though Annie had to be alive, I still felt this aching emptiness in my soul where my bond to her should have been. It was gone. Had Annie done that? Had Hera? I didn't know. I knew only that something was terribly wrong and I needed to fly.

I moved away from the crowd, not wanting to talk to anyone, swept my wings out, and took off, trying to leave the world and everything, especially my churning, consuming emotions behind. But it didn't matter how far or high I flew, I couldn't escape myself.

Movement to my left and slightly behind me caught my attention and I turned my head to see an *aurai* shadowing me a few body lengths behind and above me.

My frustration twisted into rage. I wanted to be alone. If I'd wanted to talk with someone, I would have gone over to the group of strangers and said something.

As if looking at him gave him permission to speak to me, he flapped his larger, squarer wings, and leveled out next to me.

"Glorious day!" he called out.

Was it? It didn't feel like it even though I could still fly.

I was sure I didn't know him, but I nodded an acknowledgment, not wanting to be rude. "It is, yes. But I'd like to be alone if possible."

"I was told to keep an eye on you. Something about you having a rough time in the other world and people being worried about you." The *aurai* shrugged. "But if all you needed was some space, I can give that to you. Just don't throw yourself into the ground or anything." He peeled away, slowly soaring higher, off over the seas.

Who'd told him to keep an eye on me?

At least the *aurai* had seemed to understand that I needed some space. Apparently, there were others who were worried about me. I guess that didn't surprise me. I was worried about myself.

A shudder wracked through me and I fell a few feet, my wings not supporting me for a moment, before I caught myself again. It would be so very easy to just fold my wings and fall—*throw myself at the ground*, as the *aurai* had put it—then there'd be nothing. Maybe I should. What did I have now? I couldn't claim to be a warrior. But

I did have friends, men who were like brothers to me, and Annie...

My chest tightened with grief. I was so empty, so hollow. The bond was gone and even though I'd been saved and returned to this world, it hadn't been restored. Why hadn't Annie rebonded with me? Perhaps I'd needed to be awake? Maybe she was rebonding with Aethan now?

My jaw tightened and tears leaked from my eyes. I couldn't forget the pain, the horror. It stuck with me like a niggling infection, poisoning my heart and soul. And where there should have been my bond with Annie to help quell these sickening memories, there was nothing.

I circled back, angling to fly inland, in hopes of seeing Annie and Aethan. My keen eyes picked them up, wandering back toward the beach.

Suddenly I needed to talk to her, needed to know what had happened, needed to have the bond restored.

I folded in my wings and dove.

Some part of me—much larger than I wanted to admit—pondered simply not reopening my wings, but I flared them out as I drew close to land, flapping them to land lightly near Annie and Aethan as they reached where the beach met the hills beyond.

"Annie," I said, but couldn't say more past the lump in my throat.

She squeezed Aethan's hand, which she'd been holding, and gave him a look. He nodded and moved off as she came to me, throwing her arms around me, holding me fiercely.

"Rion. Oh gods, I'm so sorry for..." She couldn't say it,

but I knew she was talking about what had happened, about my wings.

I still couldn't speak. I just held her as tightly as I could as well, locking our bodies together in a desperate need, as if the tightness of our grip could somehow replace what was missing.

We stayed that way for a long moment before I finally found words, though they were broken and choppy, spoken around heavy breaths and a throat choked with emotion. "The bond... I need it... I need you... I—"

"I need you too, Rion," she said squeezing me tighter for a moment before moving back enough to look up at me. "But I don't know how to reforge the bond. Del and I tried and nothing worked. I fear..."

My heart lurched, following her train of thought.

"No." I couldn't say more. All I could think of was that one word. No. No no no. There had to be a way, there had to be something we could do. If I was determined enough, I could fix everything. I had to fix everything.

Plucking her up, hands under her arms, I lifted her to kiss her. She responded in kind, our need desperate and intense, but as the kiss drew out longer and longer and no feeling came to me of the bond reforming, my soul started to tremble, threatening to shatter.

I set her down and fell to my knees head in hands. "It can't be."

Hot wet tears welled and rolled down my cheeks. I didn't care how unmanly they were. I didn't want to feel like this forever. I couldn't.

Annie knelt next to me. "There's a way. I have to

believe there is. But a simple kiss or even sex can't do it this time."

"What happened?" I managed to force out. I couldn't look at her, couldn't let her see my shame, couldn't look into her golden eyes and see the same heartache, so I focused on the ground and the patch of earth below me that was slowly soaking up my tears.

"Hera happened."

I flinched at the name, a name I never wanted to hear again.

"She took all of our bonds."

"No." I hugged myself.

"Oh, Rion, please." Annie wrapped her arms around me and held me close.

She stroked my back between my wings, but I flinched, unable to stop myself. Her touch reminded me of the horrid cuts Hera had inflicted, and I curled into her, my head on her shoulder, pulling her close—as awkward as that was with both of us kneeling.

This was all that was keeping me sane, all that was keeping me from flying back up, as high as I could, then simply falling. This embrace, her touch, her warmth, her body next to mine.

I felt a warmth flowing through me from where she held me.

Not having the words or capability to ask what that was, I guessed she was simply trying to heal me more. But the pain I felt wasn't physical. It couldn't be healed in that way. I needed my Annie back, my bond, my life and meaning, my everything!

I had to try bonding again. Looking up, I grabbed her

face and mashed my lips to hers. I needed this, couldn't live without this. I pressed us together as hard as I could. Annie squirmed. I knew this wasn't what she wanted. She was trying to push me away, trying to speak, but unable to with my lips hard on hers.

But with all the force and drive and will I possessed, there was no bond, no life, nothing.

I was a failure as a warrior and now as a mate. Except I didn't stop, couldn't stop, wouldn't stop. I just kept holding us there.

Strong, vise-like arms pulled me off Annie, and I squirmed and screamed, heaving against whoever held me

Annie fell back gasping.

"You were killing her," someone snarled. "She couldn't breathe!" I didn't quite know who or what was around me, I was losing myself. Some distant part of me registered Del's voice and Keph's arms holding me, but I couldn't make my mind work past the need to reform my bond with Annie.

"Relax, Rion. It's going to be okay. We'll find a way to make this work," Aethan said, but I couldn't relax. I was lost. The world had faded into a blur, and I was consumed with pain and emptiness.

Keph slapped me... hard. Then again.

I gasped, stunned, the tang of blood on my tongue, then he set me down, and I went limp, sitting hard on the ground, then collapsing onto my back, instinct making my wings vanish at the last second before I crushed them. I stared at the sky, feeling blood ooze down the back of my throat, everything, body, mind, and soul, numb. I was pretty sure my nose was bleeding, but I couldn't quite register it. My mind was retracting, sinking away into darkness and I let it go. I didn't want to be awake. Awake meant pain. Awake meant being without Annie.

And I couldn't be without her. I couldn't, so, I embraced the darkness, letting it consume my consciousness.

CHAPTER 16

ANNIE

"Is he okay?" I hurried over to Rion and checked him. He was unconscious with bruises showing up on his face from Keph's slaps, but other than that okay. Or at least okay physically. I pushed a little healing magic into him and faded away the bruises, but couldn't do anything else to help him.

"Sorry, I didn't know what to do," Keph said, his voice a low soft rumble. "He wasn't well, screaming and flailing like that. It seemed like the easiest way to get him to stop."

I didn't know if it was the best way, but it was the fastest. Rion had been having an all-out panic attack and I hadn't been able to break free of his grip.

I sighed heavily and sat back on my heels. I was all for a little rough play, but Rion had been so desperate, pressing so close and hard, I hadn't been able to breathe. One thing was certain, that sort of a kiss was not going to restore the bond.

"What are we going to do?" I asked of no one in particular.

The guys crouched or sat around me, looking as worried and confused as I felt.

"We haven't had any luck coming up with anything," Del said.

"Let's just remove all the variables," I said, rising quickly, and going to Keph.

Sitting on the ground, the big man was still more than half my height with his head reaching my chest.

"You're the only one I haven't kissed yet," I said, bending down to kiss him.

Nothing.

Fuck.

I hadn't really expected anything, but a small part of me had still hoped.

"That confirms it," I sighed as I straightened. "Just kissing isn't working."

Keph reached up and laid one of his massive hands gently on my arm. "It's well, Annie. We'll figure it out." His deep voice was still low and soft, as if he was trying to be reassuring, but I was starting to get antsy again. I'd thought I'd gotten all my anger and frustration and pent-up agitation out while riding Aethan, but it was beginning to return, and I could completely sympathize with Rion's breakdown.

"Perhaps we need an outside perspective," I said softly.

"Oh?" Del asked.

I turned to him, thinking as I spoke. "You three stay here and watch over Rion. See if you can come up with anything. I'm going to have a talk with someone who doesn't know anything about bonding." I shrugged. "We've tried everything else, so why not."

They seemed reluctant to let me go, but they all nodded and I went off to find Janice.

She and Naz stood a short distance away from the others, who were mostly grouped up on the beach, quietly talking with each other.

Evening was falling, the last remains of another stunning sunset coloring the sky, and I was getting hungry. It looked—and smelled like—someone, most likely the tritons, had done some fishing and were cooking their catch over the fire. But my bonds were more important so I continued toward Janice and ignored my stomach.

"Janice?" I asked.

She turned and looked at me, a hint of blush coloring her cheeks and making me smile. The woman still seemed out-of-sorts around men.

"I'll grab some food for us," Naz said.

"Thanks," she said to him before turning back to me. "Is it easy for you to just... bare it all, now?" Her gaze swept over me. I hadn't even really registered that I was naked. I'd woken up clothed, felt far too warm, and had simply taken everything off, then hadn't thought of it.

"I guess so," I said, giving Janice a once-over in return.

She still wore her pants and a light shirt—whatever courage she'd had for her mostly-naked trip into Masia now gone—and had probably been warm when the sun had been out.

"Naz says it's mysterious and alluring when I wear

clothes." Her gaze dipped down at herself. "Even these clothes. I don't get it. This place is... odd."

"You will, in time. Can I talk to you about something?" I asked moving closer and lowering my voice.

"Sure. What is it?"

I drew her a little farther away from the others, and we sat, our legs stretched out, our toes dipped in the warm water where the edge of the surf lapped the beach.

"Do you know anything about the magical bonding that happens in this world?" I figured I'd just go ahead and start there.

Her blank stare with one raised brow was answer enough.

"Yeah, didn't think so." I pulled up my feet a little, letting my toes play in the damp sand as I hugged my knees. "It's what happened between me and my guys. We were... connected in some deep spiritual way and because of that I could use their super-powers."

Her other brow rose.

"Hera took that away from me and now I can't seem to get it back."

"What happened?" she asked.

"Just before she tossed us out the window, she... I don't know... she touched me and... it felt like she was tearing the life out of me. But it wasn't my life. It was my bond with the guys. Except it was so much a part of me it felt like she was ripping out my heart, my soul."

"Fuck," Janice breathed. "That's awful."

"Yeah." I shook my head. "Now it's gone." I put my chin on my knees. "Before, we just had to kiss and that was it. Kissing on the lips means so much more here than it does for us, and somehow that connected me and the guys. But now that doesn't seem to work anymore."

"Kissing?"

I gave a short laugh. "Yeah, I know right? Apparently people on this world don't kiss on the lips, not unless they're deathly serious about each other. That's what signifies a bond between them. It would be like a guy giving you a ring in our world."

"Really? Wow. And when they do it, magical stuff happens?"

"Ah... well no. Not for normal people of this world. I think magical stuff only happened for me because I'm from our world? Or perhaps, I'm special somehow?"

"That you are," she said, a hint of a smile tugging at her lips, and she pulled her knees up, hugged them, and set her chin upon them, mirroring me.

"Well anyway, that doesn't work now. I've tried kissing them, I've tried... other forms of intimacy?"

"Like when you and Del fucked your brains out at the safe house?"

"You heard that?" Gods, I was so embarrassed.

"Oh, yeah. Howling monkeys in heat don't make as much noise as you do." She grinned, her smile breaking through.

Heat flushed my cheeks and I was sure I turned beat red and could only hope she wouldn't be able to see it in the growing darkness.

"Sorry, didn't mean to embarrass you. It was a joke, nothing more." Apparently, she could see just fine.

I drew in a long breath to try to get back some sense

of balance. "Anyway, nothing's worked. The bond won't come back."

"Ah."

"And I'd hoped talking to you about it would help me figure something out, but this isn't working. So I should just—" I began to rise, but Janice reached out and grabbed my shoulder sitting me back down.

"Annie, I'm sorry. I'll stop making fun and listen. I want to help, if I can."

"Thank you." I resumed my previous position, hugging my knees.

"So, what have you tried?" I could tell she was trying very hard not to grin again. "Be specific." A giggle broke through and she sucked in a sharp breath, trying to get it under control. "It's okay. Don't be embarrassed. I'll just listen, no comments."

I told her the various things I'd tried with the guys. Her eyes widened a bit at some of my explanations, but she was true to her word and kept silent. When I was done, she nodded.

"It seems you have been... thorough." But then she quirked her head to one side. "Though there *is* something you haven't tried."

"Oh?" I was quite curious. "What?"

"Some other guy."

"No," I said instantly. "I don't want a bond with some other random guy."

She sighed. "I get that, but if you *did* kiss a different guy and a bond formed that would tell us whether or not you could form one at all, or if you just can't form one with your guys. That's a distinction that's worth noting."

She was right. But still— "I don't want to risk bonding with some guy I don't care about. That almost seems worse than living without the bonds." My shoulders fell. "But you're not wrong. I just don't know how to test your theory."

We sat in silence for a long moment.

Janice finally spoke, a bit hesitant. "Ah... you could... kiss me?"

I looked at her, one brow raised. "I'm not..."

"No, I'm not really into that either, but... we're friends, yes? It wouldn't be horrible to be bound to each other would it?"

I drew in a long breath. She wasn't wrong. Still, I hesitated. Were we friends? We'd only known each other a short time, but a lot had happened in that time and we were fast becoming dear friends.

There was a certain connection between us already, just knowing about this other world and the strange things that were happening because of it.

She blew out a breath. "Yeah, sorry, bad idea. I'll—"

"No, it's not a horrible idea," I said cutting her off. "Just give me a moment to think about it?"

"Yeah, sure."

"I don't even know if the bond would work with a woman," I mused.

"Exactly."

I sighed. She was right. It was a way to test the theory and it wouldn't be the worst thing. "Let's do it."

There was an awkward moment as we tried to figure out how to just... be close.

"How about we stand," she offered. "It might be easier that way."

"Yeah."

We stood, then stared at each other for another long, awkward moment.

"I guess, we just… kiss, then?" she said.

"Yeah." I was still having second thoughts and my mind was whirling. What if it worked? Would it work? Janice was from my world not this one. Did that make a difference?

Man, I didn't know anything about these bonds other than I'd had them and lost them and desperately wanted them back.

She stepped in, laying a hand on my shoulder, an understanding look on her face. "Annie, you are a dear friend, and dear friends can sometimes kiss." Her eyes softened and she drew a bit closer.

I leaned forward a bit as did she, her hand softly sliding up from my shoulder to my jaw as our lips met.

It was a new experience for me. Her lips were softer than the guys, more tentative. I kept thinking, *she's a dear friend. I love her—in a best friend sort of way—a dear friend*.

The kiss lingered, somehow no longer feeling awkward now that our lips were pressed together. I had my eyes closed, and in some ways, it felt like kissing anyone really. I stepped in and embraced her as our lips began to part, but then…

I felt a flicker of something.

"Oh!" Janice said, our lips still close.

I opened my eyes to see her blinking, but this close all I saw was one large eye.

"You felt that too?" I asked.

It hadn't felt like it had with the guys. This had been different.

My connection to them had been a whole body feeling... I think—it was hard to recall now that I'd been without it for a while—and with her it was a spot of warmth in my chest. I didn't know what that meant, but if she'd felt it too, it had to mean something.

"I did." She drew in a long breath.

We remained there, close, as we both took a moment to understand what had happened. Then Janice dipped forward and pressed her lips to mine again, the kiss becoming a bit more impassioned. A strange new connection started to unfurl, warm around my heart, then I felt a full and resounding vibration through my soul, like I was a gong, and I'd just been rung.

Janice broke off and immediately backed away.

"Oh, wow!" she gasped. "Wow." She reached up and touched her lips. "That was..."

Telling.

So, I *could* create new bonds.

Though what I'd just formed with Janice didn't feel like what I'd shared with my guys. It *was* a bond. But it was different, not as consuming, not as soul deep. A bond of friendship perhaps?

I touched my lips as well.

Janice was staring at her fingers, the ones she'd pressed against her lips. "I hadn't expected..."

Neither had I.

"I feel..." She looked up at me. "I feel powerful!"

I wasn't quite sure what that meant.

She turned away and began to frantically search the beach. I just watched her, curious what she was thinking. She plucked up something and returned to me. She held a broken shell in her hand.

Her eyes met mine for a long moment, then she looked down, pressing the shell into her palm, drawing blood.

"Oh, what...?" I was too shocked to do anything. I didn't have a clue what she was doing.

Then she closed her eyes and drew in a breath... and the small cut healed itself, closing up.

She had my healing powers!

"Fuuuuuck," I breathed, drawing out the word in astonishment.

She opened her eyes and looked at me. "Yeah... exactly. I'd say we shared something, all right!"

CHAPTER 17

ANNIE

I DIDN'T KNOW WHAT IT MEANT. MY FIRST THOUGHT WAS... did I still have my healing powers? Had she somehow taken them from me?

I grabbed the bit of shell from her hand and did the same thing, cutting my palm. I didn't even have to close my eyes. I summoned my healing, second nature to me now, and the wound closed.

"Oh, good."

Janice quirked a brow. "You thought I'd stolen your powers?"

I shrugged. "I don't know what to think. This is new. Even the guys never shared my powers, but Hera said she could take them from those she bonded with."

"Ah." Janice nodded. "I wish I knew what to say, but I don't."

"Well, we can be certain that something happened and that I can still bond. But to be clear, this doesn't feel like what I shared with the guys. This is different."

"Oh? Really?" She looked away. "I can't stop shaking.

I'm trembling. I feel like I need to run a mile or something! Is this what you feel like all the time?"

"Not at all, no."

"So, what does that tell us?" She began to pace.

"I don't really know. I can bond, but this was different.
So… does that mean I can still bond with the guys? I have
no clue."

"Yeah, I guess this wasn't that helpful. Well, it was for
me. I feel great, but for you, not so much. Sorry." She was
rambling and I could tell she was agitated, though apparently not in a bad way. She suddenly stopped pacing. "I
wonder…"

"What?"

She didn't answer. Instead she marched away
suddenly. I followed. Despite being taller than her with
my slightly longer legs, I had to jog to keep up with her
fast pace.

"Janice?"

"I was just thinking that if I have your healing powers,
perhaps there are other things I can do now," she said,
her words coming out in a rush.

"Such as?" But then I realized where we were heading. Janice was making a bee-line straight for the stone…
the portal. "You think you can open the portal?"

She shrugged. "Don't know. Thought I'd check."

I didn't know what to say. I was fairly certain the
transfer of power hadn't gone that far, but I really didn't
know for certain.

She reached the stone. "How do you do this?" she
asked, leaning forward a bit.

Her hand hit the stone, or should have hit the stone,

but it wasn't solid anymore and she fell through the portal.

"I guess that answers that," I muttered.

Janice came scrambling back through, on all fours, her eyes wide with surprise. "Holy fuck!"

"What happened?" I asked.

"Heal me," she gasped. "I was shot and..." I knelt next to her and put a hand on her arm but couldn't sense any wounds.

"They missed you," I said.

"No." She grabbed her shirt, showing me three holes in it that hadn't been there before. "They hit, I felt it..." She lifted the shirt. The skin beneath was fine, unmarked, not even a drop of blood. "But..."

For a second I thought maybe the shots might have gone through her shirt and out the other side, missing her or grazing her and that's what she'd felt, but when she laid her shirt back, it was fairly tight on her torso and those shots—the holes in her shirt—were right on her stomach.

She kept lifting the shirt to check. "There's no blood, no holes. How is there no blood?"

"You're bulletproof?" I asked. It seemed crazy at first, but then I remembered she was at least part *aurai*, from this world, and that would mean in the other world—earth—she'd have powers. "You must be, that's your power in our world!"

"Ah... no, it isn't. I've been shot before and it was painful and bloody and horrible. Not bulletproof. But..." She kept putting her shirt down, then lifting it. "I can't explain this." She looked at me. "Maybe you're bulletproof?"

"Oh no. I can heal, but I'm sure I was shot when we came through the portal the last time. Are Hera's men still out there?"

"Yep."

"That's going to make going back tough."

"Yeah," Janice replied, her expression a mix of shock and grim resignation. She sat in the sand and took several long breaths. Finally, she looked at me. "This is fucked up."

I couldn't argue that point.

I'd hoped talking to Janice would help me figure things out, but now I was just more confused than ever.

I'd bonded with Janice.

But it was a very different kind of bonding than the one I'd had with the guys, and she now shared my powers and could open gates.

Except what did that mean?

I had no idea.

I double checked that I could still open the portal and yes, I could, confirming that she hadn't taken my powers. Which meant she shared them? Was that all that had happened for the bond? I didn't know. If she had a power, I didn't know what it might be, so I didn't know if I shared it as well. Her wings and flight were innate to her, not a power, just like my guys' shifting abilities, and she didn't seem to think she was bulletproof.

"Are you sure you don't have any powers in our world?" I asked.

She shrugged. "No clue." So, if she did, she didn't

know what it was. Though... something had happened with those bullets. But what?

Fuck! I had too many questions and not enough answers.

I thanked Janice for all her help and returned to the guys. They had a meal waiting and I hunkered down and ate in silence, my thoughts spinning. Thankfully they didn't ask about what I'd been up to and I guess my demeanor was clearly saying, 'don't talk to me now.'

I didn't even really know what I'd eaten I was so distracted, and didn't register much of anything until I put down the plate—

Plate?

"Where did we get this from?" I asked.

"A group went to Masia to collect supplies this afternoon," Aethan answered.

Right. Of course. There were more of us than just my guys and Janice and they were more than capable of taking care of themselves.

I glanced at my guys. Their expressions were all tight with worry, with the exception of Rion, who was still unconscious. Which was probably for the best since I didn't want him freaking out again. And despite that, none of them of asked about what I had or hadn't figured out when I'd gone off to talk with Janice.

I sighed. "I'm sorry, guys. I found some things out, but I only have more questions now and I don't even know if I got any answers." I grimaced and put my head in my hands. A large hand settled softly on my back and began rubbing slow circles. Keph.

"If you'd like, you can tell us what you found out, and

perhaps we might have a different thought on it?" Aethan sounded hopeful.

I sighed again and nodded, drawing my gaze back up to him. "Yeah, you're right. Maybe, if we keep talking this through and experimenting, we'll get somewhere." Blowing out a breath, I told them of my talk with Janice and the ensuing—if different—bonding with her.

"You say you don't know how it was different. Can you try to describe it?" Del asked.

"Sure." I dug my toes into the sand stared at the fire, comparing the bonding with Janice to my bonding with them.

It was only then that something clicked for me. "Oh!"

"What? Del asked.

"I just realized, and this is going to sound bad, don't take it the wrong way, but... when I bonded with Janice, I felt this deep and resounding vibration within me."

"Yes, that's what we felt," Aethan said.

"But that's just it," I said. "When I bonded with you, I don't think I felt much at all." I scoured my memories. Those times were a bit fuzzy for me, but there had been something. "There was... it felt like a shock on my lips, and a warmth in my soul, but it hadn't been much more than that, not in the initial moment of bonding. Afterward, I'd felt the connection to you all and felt it grow over time, but in that bonding moment, well, what I felt with you wasn't the same as what I felt with Janice. That might mean something." I wasn't sure what it meant, but it felt significant.

"You didn't feel something?" Aethan asked, sounding a bit put out.

I smiled. "Well, yeah. I mean, I felt things afterward. I came to feel connected with you all, I could... sense you, how you were feeling, and there was a..." How could I describe it? "There was a sort of tingling sensation at times, which I knew was my connection with you. So, there was something, but in that first moment, the actual bonding kiss, I didn't feel too much beyond the kiss." My grin turned a little sloppy. "And all the wonderful sensations that went along with it."

"Oh," Del said softly. "What I felt was like..."

"Like a bell rang in my soul," Keph finished.

"Yeah," Aethan agreed. "It shook me and resonated within me. It felt amazing!"

"That's what I felt when I bonded with Janice," I said excitedly. Though I could see they still weren't thrilled to hear I'd had more of a reaction to her than I'd had to them. I pushed on. "And it sounded like Janice felt something like that as well. So, I guess the other end of the bonding was the same. I don't know why I felt something with her and not you guys."

"Did you do anything different with her than you did with us?" Aethan asked.

Another good question. I thought about it.

Here again, remembering back to my first bonding with the guys—and I don't know why I hadn't thought of this earlier—I recalled that there had been words, a ritual that had gone with it. With Rion, it had been short and sweet, but with the others I'd drawn it out, made it a formal thing, like wedding vows. How had I forgotten that?

"Yeah, there was a difference, a lot of difference in how it happened…" Now that I thought about it, I felt like I was on the verge of a realization and excitement bubbled within me. "With you all there had been a ritual. I'd asked if you wanted to bond—though in Rion's case he'd been the one asking and I'd accepted. But there had been that verbal agreement before we did it. With Janice there wasn't anything like that. We talked about it, but then just did it. We… Oh wait!" That was interesting. We *had* talked about being friends and being bonded and how that wouldn't be the worst thing. And I'd been thinking about my sisterly love for her when we'd bonded. So…

"What?" Aethan asked, his eyes bright with hope.

How could I put this into words? My thoughts were still tumbling around in my head and not quite fitting together yet. "I was thinking of bonding with her, of bonding with a friend and we'd talked about it as friends, as…" My skin tingled. "As… equals." That was it! "Perhaps that's why it affected me too! We bonded as equals. But when I bonded with you… you all still thought I was a goddess at the time, you were giving yourselves to me wholly and I was… well I was accepting that. I was taking your bond but not truly giving you mine? No, that doesn't sound quite right either, but there's something in there I think."

I trembled. I could feel the answer just out of reach. If I just stretched a little farther, just a little more… "When I tried bonding with you the second time, it wasn't the same at all. There was need and desperation, there was passion and intimacy, but there wasn't that full agreement, not like the first time. Perhaps that's essential to the bonding process?"

"Yes!" Aethan said, moving around the fire to me. "Let's try it. I, Aethan of—"

"Wait," I said holding up a hand. "That's part of it, but I don't think it's all of it. Let's not do this until we have a better idea. I don't want us all to get our hopes up and be disappointed."

Aethan stared at me, a mix of emotions flashing across his face: sadness, disappointment, hope, then he gave a tight nod. "What do you think we're missing?"

"I'm not sure," I said.

Del inched closer to me. "Let's go over it again."

"We're close," I said. I could feel it. There was just one piece to the puzzle we needed to figure out.

CHAPTER 18

KEPHAS

I felt my heart quicken at the thought that my bond with Annie might be restored. We hadn't come to a conclusion yet, but I felt like we were drawing close. After we'd gone over a few things, we had a short list of what might be required.

A formal agreement.

A mutual desire to be connected as equals.

A kiss. There had been a lot of discussion around this, about emotions as well. Apparently there had been a fair amount of intimacy between Annie and Aethan, and Annie and Del in recent times.

"I'd felt something when we kissed," she said to Del. "When we were saying goodbye on the beach, and you were going off to your home and Janice and I were headed to Masia. I think it may have been something connected to bonding."

Her expression softened and I could see her love for him in her eyes. It was a look she'd shared with us all at one point or another.

"I think perhaps that kiss was our purest, the closest we'd gotten to the state we needed to be in to bond," she continued. "Something about giving of yourself to the other without restrictions or limits. Only love."

"Yeah," Aethan murmured. "In all the turmoil and pain of the last few days. I think we've forgotten what forged our bond. It was love. Love for you and for each other. We've had so much else on our minds..." He glanced at Rion and his expression turned glum.

The *erinai* slept peacefully. I was sorry I'd had to hit him to get him to finally rest. It had been one of the most painful things I'd ever done, but I didn't think he would have stopped otherwise. He'd been beyond reason and I could only hope when he woke he'd be calmer.

I turned my attention to the sea and watched the dark waves lap against the shore in the distance. Stone Titan's had exceptional dark vision and I could see out over the waves, and the sea beyond, especially with the stars out. I couldn't look at the others for a moment. They had endured so much, while I...

Hera had been able to hurt me. She'd borrowed my own power and become strong enough to hit me so it would hurt, but that hadn't really done that much. There'd been bruises, but not much more. She'd tried using tools on me, but with how durable I was in that world, and the force she'd needed, those tools usually broke before my skin did.

She'd given up on me after a while, simply leaving me in isolation, which in itself wasn't great because I could occasionally hear the screams of Aethan and Rion, and knew they were probably taking the brunt of her frustration because I hadn't provided any outlet for the mad goddess. I hadn't had it half as bad as they did and my heart hurt with guilt about that.

"Keph?"

I turned back at Annie's voice.

"Are you okay?"

I raised a brow. "What does that mean? Okay?" I asked.

She grimaced. "Sorry, other-world-speak. Are you doing well? You seem distracted."

"I am. But don't worry about me, please. Let's go on. Where were we?" I smiled for the others, hoping to ease their worry even though I knew I wasn't really the cause of that worry.

"We think we're ready to try bonding," Annie said. Then that look of love and intensity filled her gaze as she looked at me. "And I want to try it with you first."

"Me? No, you don't have to, the others—"

"We..." She looked at the other two. "We've tried and I don't want those previous attempts to influence me. With you there haven't been previous attempts. Well, there was that one kiss from earlier, but... yeah. I don't think that really counted. I think we can do this fresh and clean and see how it works. What do you think?"

My pulse picked up.

Annie's gaze dipped to my lap, where my cock must have stirred. "Ah, I see you think this is a good idea?" she purred, a mischievous grin sparkling in her eyes. "Great. Come on, let's step away a bit and have some privacy." She rose and offered me her hand. I didn't need it, but I took it as I too rose.

I nodded to Aethan and Del, who both looked eager and a bit envious.

Annie led me into the darkness, though with my stone titan eyes, I could see well enough in the dark. We moved inland a bit until she stopped and glanced back at our fire, now a good number of paces away and partially hidden by a dune.

"I think that should be far enough." She turned to me, looking up with her heart in her eyes. "Thank you, Keph. You're always so willing to help, so kind and gentle and tenderhearted."

She stepped in and kissed my chest. This brought her body pressing close to my erection and the tip of my cock brushing the bottom of her breasts.

"Now come down here so I can kiss you," she said reaching up to cup my cheek.

I knelt, both knees on the ground, to be roughly eye-to-eye with her, and took a moment to simply take her in, appreciating her fine red-blond hair that framed a speckled face with large, soft golden-brown eyes, her wide, free smile that was always warm, and her full breasts and hips, and slender waist that made me hot with desire. She was a wonder and it was clear in the way she looked at me that she loved me as much as I loved her.

"I love you, Annie. You're..." My words vanished for a second. There was so much I wanted to say and yet none of it seemed smart enough for someone like Annie. "You're unlike any woman I've ever met. So strong and fierce, but not a warrior. You're soft and yet hard, delicate and yet strong, terrified and still brave. You're a whole lot of perfect opposites."

She huffed a soft laugh at that and stepped closer still, cupping my cheeks in her small, delicate hands. I was reminded of our first kiss in that strange closet at the conference center with Rion watching. Again, as she drew in to press close to me, she was forced to straddle my erection, and I felt her wetness as I brushed her opening. Her breath caught, then quickened as her gaze on mine became intense.

She kissed me lightly on the mouth, only a brief brush of her soft lips.

"That wasn't to bond," she murmured, "that was just... for you being you." Then she swallowed hard and a hint of fear and need darkened the softness in her gaze. "Let's do this before I get too aroused and just want to ride your amazing cock."

I rumbled a laugh. "We can do both."

"Yeah, good idea, but let's do the bonding first."

I nodded.

She drew in a steadying breath, even as her hips swayed slightly, rubbing herself on my erection.

"Kephas Vathia Spiti," she began.

I was a bit surprised she recalled my clan name. Most people didn't care to remember it. Even I wasn't particularly fond of it. I thought it sounded a bit harsh. But Annie always made it sound soft and warm.

"Will you accept a bond with me, Annie Chambers? There will be no going back from this. I will be yours entirely, and you will be mine. There will be others who will join with us, and together we will be one. Equals in love, one body, one soul, one heart. Is this what your heart desires?" Her breath was heavy and hot, her face so very close to mine, so close her lips would brush mine when she spoke again. She was more than ready to go through with this and so was I.

I found my own breath catching as my heart thundered within me. This was everything I wanted. Having a woman like Annie—a woman like no other—and to be a part of something powerful with her and my truest friends.

"Yes," I breathed, my lips teasing hers. "I Kephas Vathia Spiti do wish to bond with you, Annie Chambers, for now and for always. To be one with all of those who I hold dear in this world. To that I commit my body, my heart, and my soul. One with you, equals with all."

"Wow," Annie said softly, nibbling on my bottom lip. "Let's do this." And then her lips pressed to mine.

The kiss quickly deepened as we opened to each other. She tilted her head to one side, pushing deeper still, not forceful or demanding, but insistent and loving.

And I felt something... several somethings.

My immediate physical reaction was a swelling of my cock. Annie's breath caught mid-kiss as I lifted her a little. This had happened before as well. She was making all manner of amazing noises, as her hips started rocking, moving over me.

But there was a deeper reaction as well. I felt it, soft and subtle at first, a ringing in my soul, a... knowing.

It grew, spreading through me, growing stronger, louder, ringing me like a bell. Annie seemed to undulate and tremble. Somehow, I knew I wasn't the only one feeling this ringing connection, that Annie was feeling it as well.

She pushed back, breathing hard.

"Did you feel that?" Her eyes glistened with unshed tears of joy. "Oh, Keph! It worked!" Her gaze shifted from elated to hot with passion. "Now let's get to that cock-riding."

I wanted that, intensely, but I didn't know if she was ready yet. I slid one of my arms around her, then down between her legs to the slick opening there.

She gasped as I probed and played, our kisses becoming hard and intense. She had reached down as well, grasping the end of my cock, grinding against it, pleasuring herself.

With our desperation, it wasn't long before she was crying out with her first release, her warmth rushing over my fingers and her muscles contracting then relaxing even more.

I withdrew my hand and she went to her toes to align my tip with her entrance and slowly take it into her. She was still in the throes of her first orgasm, and she gasped and trembled all the harder as I started to enter her.

"Oh Gods, yes!" she breathed. She kissed me, hot and wet and hard. "I want you, all of you, inside me."

I wasn't sure if that was a good idea. There weren't many women her size who could fit all of me. But even as I considered what to say, she was slipping farther down on me, taking more of me into her than she had before.

I grabbed her butt with one large hand and her back with the other, cradling her. She rose a bit and wrapped her legs around me, and I crouched a little so she could rest her legs on my thighs, laying her back a little as I took control, slowly pushing deeper within her. She threw her head back, mouth open and gasping as I did.

It took a long time, a long and painfully slow time, since I didn't want to hurt her. And I grew more and more surprised that I *wasn't* hurting her. In fact, she seemed lost in bliss, eyelids half closed and fluttering as her body twitched and trembled. She let out low deep moans and sharp cries of pleasure. I hit a spot where I didn't think I could go deeper, but it was Annie who pulled herself down with her legs, clasped around my thighs, past that point and farther.

Then, somehow, I was fully inside of her.

She didn't even seem to realize how astonishing this was and simply began grinding herself upon my base, gasping and letting out high keening noises.

I began slow, careful thrusts. Usually I wouldn't even dare such a thing, letting the woman do all the movement, just to be safe, but with Annie... Perhaps our bonding had truly changed us, and made this possible.

"Yes, harder," she gasped, voice hoarse. Her skin was glistening, the moonlight catching in her sweat, and she slid her hands up her body and fondled her own breasts, squeezing them, ratchetting up her pleasure. I wished those were my hands, and from her hot and mischievous look, I think she knew it. Except I was supporting her. She lay upon my hands like a bed as I bent over her and... as asked... I began to pick up my pace.

Then her hands moved up, to tangle in her hair as her gaze went from playful to eye-rolling bliss. I moved her over my erection with ever quicker and harder thrusts, losing myself in passion, which I'd so rarely been able to achieve.

"Yes," I grunted. This was so new for me, it was astounding and exciting and amazing.

"Yes!" she echoed, crying out into the night with all her heart and soul, her body arching back, stiff and trembling as she convulsed in the throes of another orgasm.

I was lost in the pleasure now. I didn't know how this was possible, to be so hard and needful and rough with a woman and not... break her. But with Annie, it seemed anything was possible.

"Come," Annie breathed, her gaze catching mine. "I want to feel you come." Even amidst her current peak, it seemed she was aching for more.

I didn't need any more of an invitation. I was ready and I let out a feral roar as I released within her.

"Holy, fuuuu..." she cried out, voice rising in pitch. Her eyes rolled up as she shook wildly in my grasp, but I made sure she didn't fall as we came together—violently and far too loudly—in the night.

CHAPTER 19

ANNIE

I LAY, STARING UP AT THE STARS, MY BODY TINGLING AND alive. I'd never felt so amazing before, but then, I'd never had sex like that before either.

I couldn't quite explain how it felt with Keph, like my body had somehow adapted to his, opening more, taking him in deeper. I hadn't thought I could take him fully inside me, but apparently I'd been wrong. He'd gotten as far as I thought he could go, but I'd wanted more, and with my legs hooked over his, I'd pulled myself down, experimenting, and I think I'd surprised us both when that had worked.

I still didn't quite believe it. Nor did I believe how much he'd let loose, unrestrained and hard. It had literally shaken me to my core, but in a good, amazing way, in the amazing raw power mixed with tenderness way which was sex with Keph.

On top of that was our bonding moments before. Just the memory of that mind-blowing moment made my whole body tingle.

"I felt that," Keph said, a low, soft rumble. He sat next to me, his legs pulled up, head resting on the bulge of a muscled arm atop his knees, looking at me.

"And I felt you," I whispered, referring to our time together. So deep and large and hard and wonderful.

He chuckled again.

"Holy fuck," I giggled. It *had* been a rather divine fuck after all.

I didn't even know if I'd be able to walk! Though, I felt... fine. More than fine. I felt incredible!

When he'd withdrawn from me, I'd felt a moment of being hollow, but then that had faded and I'd seemed to... shift.

I couldn't explain how it felt. It was like I'd somehow adjusted to fit him, then once he was gone, I'd gone back to how I was. Except, that didn't make any sense at all. How could I do that? I wasn't even really sure it had happened. I'd have to have more sex with Keph to find out. And that seemed like a very good idea... but later.

Right now, I was exhausted from a long and draining day and from truly world-shattering sex with this amazing man.

I began to rise and Keph moved quickly to help me up, but I didn't need help. There wasn't any soreness or stiffness, no awkward bow-legged wobbling. I was strong and firm.

"Holy fuck," I whispered again. I felt like I should be as awkward as a newborn foal, but I wasn't. What I was, was tingling and so very satisfied. So, I just kept whispering, "holy fuck." Then we both giggled, Keph's a low rumbling from deep within him.

We made our way back to the others and Aethan came running up to us.

"Did..." He blinked, perhaps noticing the blissful looks on both our faces. "It worked? It worked!"

"Yes," I replied.

"I told him as much," Del said strolling up to us. "You two certainly made a racket out there. I figured that wouldn't have happened if you'd failed."

"And I told him you were just too hot and no man would be able to resist you, success or failure. Perhaps he was consoling you," Aethan shot back with a grin.

I laughed. "Yes, it worked. We're bonded, and you two are next." I was tired, yes, but also felt like I wouldn't be able to sleep just yet. Perhaps more mind-blowing sex would do it.

Del gave a relieved laugh. "Aethan, you can go first, if you like."

"I would yes," he said. "That's big of you."

I gave Keph a look. He nodded. There was an understanding between us now, like there had been before—a knowing of how each other was feeling—and he sat at the edge of the fire, peaceful and still. He'd rest well tonight.

As would I, eventually.

I took Aethan's offered hand and we moved away from the others. I could practically feel the excited energy radiating off him. He was like a kid on Christmas morning.

And he should be... I was quite the present.

I gave a short laugh. Thoughts like that, so confident

and empowered, had been so rare and fleeting for me since I'd lost the bond.

"What?" Aethan asked.

"Nothing. I'm just feeling a whole lot better than I was."

He nodded. "Earlier, when we went for a ride, you were..."

"Lost, desperate, confused, terrified, dejected?" I said, shooting off the list, the words rushing out.

"Yeah." He squeezed my hand, his expression softening and turning serious. "I'm glad you're feeling better."

I stopped, turning to him. "Shall we?"

He nodded, energy and enthusiasm in his eyes, but his body was still. "Guide me."

Of all my guys, he was the closest to my height, just a hair shorter than I was. I stepped in, cupped his face with both hands, and brought him close but didn't kiss him. Instead, I rested my forehead on his.

"Aethan of the Theophylian Plains," I whispered, my own hot breath washing back upon me.

I was going to say what I said for Keph, but realized those words would be a disservice to Aethan, to all of them. This needed a unique touch. And I knew just what Aethan needed. Of all my guys, he had been the least confident, the least self-assured.

"You are an amazing partner," I said. "Always there to help, whether it's me or any of the others. You're a dedicated friend and a giving lover."

He let out a shuddering breath, not of impassioned heat, but close to tears. "Thank you," he murmured.

"Never doubt yourself, Aethan. I don't doubt you. I love you, deeply and truly." I quirked a smile as my mind turned a little dirty. For some reason, with him, it seemed fitting. "Every time your cock has been inside me, I've hit incredible heights of passion. I can't wait to have it again." I reached down and ran two fingers along the top of his rigid erection, and drew my lips to his, nipping his lower lip.

"Oh?" he breathed, his body trembling.

"Oh, yes." I gave a breathy laugh. "And I know you have such incredible patience and control as a lover. But I won't prolong this any more than I have to." I cleared my throat. "Will you accept my bond, Aethan? This is a final and binding seal between us. We, together with the others, will be one in body and heart and soul. We'll be equals. Do you hear that? You and I, and the others, will be equals. No more worshiping me." I gave another quick laugh. "Unless I'm worshiping you too. This is my bond. Do you accept it?"

A tribute to his patience, he didn't respond right away.

Everything that I'd said had been true, no exaggeration or lies. I needed this to be a pure moment and it was, and I think he was soaking it all in.

"Annie," he began softly, slowly, bringing a hand to my waist as if to help steady me. "I love you with all my heart and soul and being. And I love Del and Keph and Rion dearly as well. There is nothing more in this world —" He gave his own quick laugh. "—or any other, that I want more than to be one with you and them. I give myself to you, and to them, heart and soul and body. And

I accept you, and them, as equals." He paused. "Equals," he repeated with more confidence as if he'd needed to see that truth and finally had.

Good.

I lowered my lips to his, teasing, tasting them tentatively, before pushing deeper. He too played and teased before our mouths—and souls—opened to each other.

It came slowly, building, radiating out from my core to my entire body, that resonant vibration. I shook and felt him shake in tune with me. And as that bond formed and deepened, so too did our kiss.

My arms encircled his neck as he pressed a hand against the small of my back and pulled me closer. His other hand, the one on my waist, slid up my side and cupped my breast.

I pushed my belly hard against his, capturing his cock between us, and sensed his passion, love, and burning desire, as I opened my own emotions up to him.

When our lips finally separated, I brushed mine along his cheek, pressing close as I whispered into his ear, "This afternoon I took you. Since we're now equals, I think it's time you took me just as hard."

"Yes, my goddess," he whispered back. I was just about to chide him for 'worshiping' me when he then said, "I'll be your god."

That was more like it.

He spun me around roughly. I was a bit surprised and gave a clipped cry of confusion and excitement. His hands, firm and forceful on my hips, pressed me to him, his erection between my ass cheeks. Then he slid his hands over my waist and sides, and around to my breasts, grasping, holding, fondling, owning.

I moaned and relaxed back onto him, grinding my butt against his cock as forceful as he kneaded my breasts, my need to have him inside me swelling. I ached for him, but not with the heartbreaking emptiness of before. This was deep, throbbing desire born from the renewed connection between our souls.

He trailed a hand down my belly, skimming my abs, teasing into my curls, and dipping into my wet folds. A whisper of a climax teased through me as he dipped his fingers in my wetness and teased it over my clit.

Oh, yes.

I ground back against him, savoring the delicious torture of his fingers on my clit and inside me, working me up.

Then he shifted, bending his knees to slid the tip of his cock up between my legs. He teased my entrance, his fingers helping to guide him to where I needed him, sending another whispering climax rushing through me.

"Yes," I moaned, desperate to have him inside me.

But he continued to tease me, shallowly pushing inside me then withdrawing, again and again.

Oh, God.

His hands slid to my thighs and he urge me to close them on him. Suddenly his cock felt twice as big inside me, hitting all the right places, torturing me with a glimmer of what I really wanted: him driving inside of me, riding me like I'd ridden him.

I squirmed, pushing back into him, trying to take him deeper, faster, harder.

He hummed his pleasure, a pure masculine sound of desire that sent shivers rushing over me, and pressed a hand on my back, bending me forward and making his cock hit another, incredible spot inside me.

I shuddered. This would be a core workout indeed, but God did it feel amazing.

But then his hands moved around in front of me again, helping support me, as he used my own weight to put the most divine pressure on my breasts.

He captured my hardened nipples between his thumbs and forefingers, pulling and pressing, sending spikes of pleasureful-pain as he slowly moved inside me, working up, building me to a soft, exquisite climax that was wonderful, but not at all what I craved.

"Aethan," I moaned. "Please."

"I can't have you coming just once," he said.

I huffed. "I'm beginning to regret praising your patience as a lover."

"You did want me to take control."

"Not that kind of control."

He chuckled, the sound low and sensual, seized my hips, and thrust into me.

The impact sent a shuddering after shock rushing through me and stole my breath in the most delicious way.

I opened my mouth to encourage him, but he jerked halfway out and thrust back in, just as hard, then repeated the action again and again. His pace was hard and fast, his fingers digging into my skin. I gasped and cried my pleasure as he pounded into me.

He grunted as he jerked my hips back to meet his

powerful thrusts. Our bodies crashed together, the sound of flesh slapping against flesh joining our gasps and moans, and my desire twisted tighter and tighter.

This was what I wanted, what I needed.

It was perfect and wonderful, and felt so much better than the last time because our souls were bonded together again.

His thrusts grew wild and with a feral scream, he slammed a final thrust home, hitting the perfect spot inside me and sending me crashing over the edge.

All my muscles contracted and I screamed my release. He grabbed my chest and hauled me up, clutching me against his body, as our orgasms tore through us, wave after wave of glorious, trembling muscle contractions.

We stayed, frozen and trembling, in that position for some time, until we were both spent, then he eased his iron grip, but still kept his arms around me.

"Ohhhhh," he drew out the word, and I felt one final shudder rush from him, then he slowly pulled out of me.

I turned quickly and pressed myself to him, kissing him intently. "That was amazing," I whispered. "Thank you, my god."

He smiled and touched my cheek, freeing some hair plastered by sweat, brushing it behind my ear. "Anytime, my goddess. I will always be here for you."

CHAPTER 20

DELPHON

ANNIE WAS FLUSHED, HER HAIR WILD, AS SHE AND AETHAN returned to the light of the fire, making me smile. I was happy for Aethan and Keph. I'd had Annie all to myself these last few days while they'd been in a much worse situation. They needed this, and so did Annie.

Aethan nodded to me with a confident grin as he sat at the fire beside Keph, and Annie came to me.

"Your turn." She sounded tired and a little drunk. After what I'd just heard in the night from her times with Keph and Aethan, I could understand her slightly giddy nature.

"Come," I said softly. I swept her into my arms and had been about to say 'let me carry you,' but she spoke first.

"Oh, I have. Lots of times." She giggled. "Are you going to give me more?"

Except even as she said this, she snuggled against my chest, her eyelids drooping as I walked away from the others to give us privacy.

"Perhaps," was my only reply. It hadn't been my intent to pleasure her, only to rebond with her, but we'd see how things played out.

She seemed semi-delirious, dozing as I carried her past the larger camp of the others who'd helped us rescue Rion, Aethan, and Keph to the water's edge. There I laid her gently in the shallow waters, angled so her head would be on the beach above the waves but her legs would be well in the surf.

"Oh," she murmured, her eyelids flickering open. "Water?"

"Yes," I laughed. "I figured you could use a nice warm bath after your... escapades."

"Oh?" she said, blinking, then she relaxed. "Yeah, that would be lovely."

I caressed her, moving the water over her, using a bit of sand to softly scrub some less-sensitive places, starting with her legs and slowly moving up. Once I reached places where the water didn't lap around her, I cupped it in my hands and brought it to pour over her: belly, breasts, then carefully rinsed her shoulders, face, and hair.

"Hmmmm," she said, her lids starting to slid shut again. "We should bond before you put me to sleep."

"I can wait if you need the rest."

Her lids snapped open at that and I could see the heartache of our broken bond in her eyes. "I can't wait. Even if I need the rest."

"I understand." I lay on my side next to her, propped up on one arm. My other hand traced delicate patterns on her stomach and occasionally up around her breasts or down over her hips. "Go ahead," I murmured.

She drew in a long breath, letting out a contented sigh. "Thank you for that. Now, to mix some business with our pleasure. Delphon of Galniosia, will you bond with me?"

"I will," I said softly

She blinked and laughed, "I wasn't done yet!"

"Oh, go on."

She slid an arm under where I was propped up and snuggled closer to me. "Where was I? Right. Delphon of Galniosia, will you bond with me?" She shot a sidelong look at me, and I pressed my lips tight in a promise that I wouldn't interrupt her again. "This is an irrevolvable... irrevobakle... irrerev..." She paused, drew a breath. "This is a binding bond..." She giggled. "I'm getting so tired I don't quite have the words. Let me say this simply. I love you, Del. I love you and all the others with all my heart and soul and body... especially my body." Another giggle. "The bond will make sure that we are one, all of us are one, equal in all things. Is that what you want? If so... kiss me." She grinned.

"Annie of Chicago, yes. All I want is to be one with you and the others. I want to be one in body and soul and heart, equal with you and them, together forever, bound and committed. I'm yours and you are mine. We are theirs and they are ours. This is my pact and bond with you." I lowered myself, leaning over her. But I stopped before my lips touched hers. "I love you, Annie."

"I love you too, Del," she said, all giddiness gone, her gaze intense and solemn.

I kissed her softly, gently. Slowly, we opened to each other, though there wasn't any hard passion, just tenderness and love, and I felt my body tremble as the bonding took me.

It was soft at first, like our kiss, but then grew and spread, rocking me with its intense vibration.

Annie was trembling too, moaning softly, her breath picking up, chest heaving.

We shook together as the bond solidified, then quieted. I could feel her exhaustion and relief.

Lifting back a bit, I asked, "We've bonded. What would you like now?" My hand went back to tracing soft patterns on her belly.

"Stay close," she whispered, sleepily. Then she lifted her head—it seemed to take some effort—to look at the waves upon her lower body. "Make sure I don't drown. I want to fall asleep in your arms."

That was fair.

I pulled her close, rolling her a little to lay atop me, my chest as her pillow even though the tide was going out and there was little chance she'd drown before she woke. I stroked her back, washing off the sand, then held her. Her breathing quieted and evened out, and then she started snoring.

I smiled. I was dedicated to her now, snoring and all. I drifted off as well, eyes closing on the star-splashed sky above feeling complete and whole.

I woke to water lapping against my toes and opened my eyes, immediately regretting it as the sun blinded me.

Wincing, I blinked, but couldn't raise an arm to shield

my eyes as both were pinned down by Annie. She lay atop one of them and was reaching over, holding the other, and if I moved, I could wake her, and she'd had a... busy night.

Instead I rolled my head to one side, blinking until my vision normalized. It was only then that I saw Aethan sitting on the sands not far away, his knees pulled up, his chin resting on them.

"Morning," I whispered.

He looked over, noting me and the still sleeping Annie, and smiled. "I was sent to find you and tell you we have a meal prepared when you're ready." He kept his voice low, then he rose and left.

The tide was coming in, which meant we had slept for nearly twelve hours.

My stomach rumbled.

Then Annie's rumbled, sounding even more empty than mine, and she squirmed, starting to wake.

I kissed the top of her head. "Morning, my love."

She groaned. "I have sand everywhere."

"That's what happens when you sleep on a beach. Luckily there's a sea nearby where you can wash it off. Shall I bathe you again?"

"Oooh," she said, her squirms gaining more energy. "That was nice. So relaxing." She shifted raising herself up a little to look at me. "But I think that's part of what got sand everywhere." She blew a few strands of hair from her face. "It's in my hair and in my mouth." She stuck her tongue out.

"So, is that a yes or no to a bath?"

She grinned. "A yes to having your hands all over me, a no to doing it while lying on the beach."

I returned her smile. "I can accommodate that."

We rose and I escorted her into the waves until she was chest deep. Then I washed her, moving my hands over her wonderfully speckled skin. We kissed and played, though it didn't go any further than that, before our stomachs were rumbling again.

"I'm famished," she said. Then she looked up at me, her eyes large and innocent, and fluttered her eyelashes in an over-exaggeration of innocence. "You carried me down to the beach last night. Could you carry me back? That way I won't get sand all dried up in my toes."

I scooped her up and she gave a yelp of glee.

As I carried her out of the water and back to our camp beyond the beach, she said, "You didn't get any last night. We should rectify that."

"There will be lots of time for that," I replied. "I think you need to bond with Rion first."

She nodded, face falling a little. "You're right. He wasn't doing well yesterday at all."

"No."

Once we reached the camp, I set her down and both of us were given a plate with sweet-pastries, some slices of fruit, and freshly roasted meat.

Annie quickly finished her first plate and was given more.

"How long were we down there?" she asked.

"It's past noon," Aethan said in answer. "A while."

We all looked over at Rion. He was still out cold.

"Are we sure he's well?" Keph asked.

Annie put a hand on his chest, and closed her eyes. "His body is well, and he's breathing fine. He went through a lot. Perhaps he just needs time to recover."

She went back to her meal, and we ate for a few more minutes before Aethan sighed and met all of our gazes one by one.

"Once we're all bonded again," he said, "Then what?"

Annie licked the last of the crumbs and fruit juices from her plate and set it down. "I don't know. We still have to face Hera. There's no way she'll just let us go, even if we're willing to turn a blind eye to all the horrible things she's done and will likely continue to do. But I don't know how, not yet." She smiled, despite her grim words. "But we figured out how to bond again, so I know we can figure that out, too." She rose and stretched and we all marveled at her proud, beautiful body.

She noticed us and blushed a little. "What are you all looking at?" she asked playfully.

"The most beautiful woman in the world," I said softly.

She blushed more, it spread down her neck and chest in the most alluring way. Gods, she was even more beautiful when she blushed so deeply.

She finished her stretches and turned away kneeling next to Rion. "Let's see if we can't wake him and get him bonded again." She looked back over her shoulder. "Then all four of you can... show me exactly how beautiful you think I am," she added with a wink.

Through all the bathing and intimacy last night and this morning, I hadn't truly gotten aroused, but now, with that mischievous look in her eyes, I felt my cock stir and rise.

Annie eyed me. "Exactly," she chuckled. "But first Rion!" She turned back to him and leaned down to whisper something in his ear.

CHAPTER 21

HYPERION

"I LOVE YOU, MY ANGEL," THE VOICE—ANNIE'S VOICE— filled my being and shredded the nightmares which threatened the edges of my dreams.

I drew in a long breath and opened my eyes to see Annie leaning over me. She smiled and kissed me softly. "Hello there, sleepyhead."

Instantly, I recalled how I'd forced myself on her, and my chest tightened with shame and regret.

"I'm so sorry," I said, tears coming to my eyes. I was so fragile, so confused, my soul broken, that I couldn't control myself, even if I should have. "I lost control. I still—"

"I know," she murmured, kissing the tears off my cheeks. "You were just trying so hard to get our bond back. I don't mind a little rough play. I just couldn't breathe. It's well, you're well, and..." She smiled and I felt my whole soul ease and spring to life with that look. "We know how to bring the bond back now. Would you like that?"

I nodded. More tears leaked from my eyes as my emotions welled up and overwhelmed me. "Please, yes. I need you, Annie. I'm lost without you."

She quirked an odd grin at that. "I know," she replied, pressing a hand over her heart. "I feel that way, too. Let's get you up and go for a walk."

I nodded and she leaned back so I could rise.

The other guys were all there, watching, and my face heated with shame. I turned my head away from them, not wanting them to see me like that, all those years with my father reminding me that men didn't cry, they didn't show weakness, they were strong, they didn't get taken prisoner, rushed through me.

"No," Annie said, touching my face. "There's no shame here. Tears are always welcome. Emotions are real and powerful things. We all need to be able to express them. None of this manly-man bullshit, got it?"

I nodded.

The other guys got up and surrounded me, slapping me warmly on the shoulders.

"It's well," Aethan said. "I know— well I don't know what you went through, but I know what I went through and I know that wasn't easy. But, as you're about to find out, we're stronger together. We're all here for each other. Whatever you need."

"Exactly," Annie said. "Thank you, Aethan."

Del handed me a plate of food and I ate hungrily as the others stood nearby. They all seemed to be so content and serene. I wanted that, and knew it came from being bonded with Annie again. So, I bolted down the food, handed the plate back to Del then turned to

Annie. She put a finger to my lips, perhaps seeing my desperation.

"Hush, I know." She took my hand and began to lead me away from the others. To them, she said, "Give us a little privacy, yes?"

The others went back to their fire, and Annie led me off, over the next hill into a small valley.

Then she turned to me and rested both of her hands on my chest, her expression serious. "There is something you need to hear before we bond."

My pulse stuttered. This sounded like it was going to be bad news, and I tried to brace myself, but I had no inner fortitude. I was just too broken and fragile after everything that had happened.

"What?" I asked, my voice rough and just a little too harsh.

She looked up at me, her eyes intense, but not hard, then she cupped my cheeks with her warm hands. I leaned into her palm, comforted by that touch.

"Rion," she said, "we're going to bond, never doubt that. But before we do, I wanted to ask you something."

"Yes?" I waited on a razor's edge. She said she'd bond with me, but I couldn't help but fear if I said the wrong thing, I'd ruin my chances.

"Are you whole?" she asked, her voice edge with worry and grief.

I frowned. "Whole?"

A shudder swept through me and the memory of *that woman*—I couldn't think her name—digging out my wing rushed into my mind. I'd already flown, but I still suddenly needed to know that my wing was there, that flying hadn't been a dream. I pushed them out, both of them, and stretched them out to either side.

Still there.

Thank God.

I could still fly.

I could still take Annie flying.

And yet, even knowing my wings were back, I still felt unsteady, broken.

Because I'd failed. I was the warrior among my brothers and not defeating *that woman* had been my fault.

"I know what she did," Annie murmured. "I saw. I healed you."

"Oh." I didn't recall that. There had been a hazy moment of pain fading away in a cold alley, but that was it.

She let her hands wander over me. "I'm... very aware that you're whole in body," she said with a slightly mischievous look. "I intend to test that out once we've bonded, but that wasn't what I was asking. How's your spirit?"

Ah.

For a long moment I couldn't respond, my whole body trembled with fear at what had happened, at the emptiness inside me, with the worry that Annie wouldn't accept me, no matter what she'd just said, because I wasn't the man she'd first met.

I couldn't get the memory of what *that woman* did out of my mind, and I couldn't shake the feeling that even though I had proof, my wing was still gone.

She put a hand to my cheek again. "It's okay, you can tell me."

"I—" My throat tightened. Annie wouldn't want me to lie. Even though we weren't bonded, she'd probably be able to tell if I lied. How I felt wasn't something I could hide from her or the others. They knew me too well.

"I'm a failure," I forced out, trying to swallow back a sob at saying the truth out loud. "I'm broken... and afraid."

I was a soldier. I was supposed to have become the next Sky General. And now I was nothing, terrified of ending up back in *that woman's* hands, of losing my wings for good, of losing Annie.

And while I didn't care if I was anything to my people, and I sure didn't care if I was anything to my father, it broke my heart that I was no longer a warrior for Annie.

But rebonding with her would fix that. It would make everything right. It had to.

"I'm—" Tears burned my eyes and I clenched my jaw, fighting to hold it in, unable to resist what had been beaten into me as a child.

"It's okay," she murmured. "Just sit with me."

She guided me to the ground. I made my wings vanish to make it easier to sit, and she wrapped her arms around me, holding me close.

"I know that wasn't easy to say. And I'm sorry I had to make you say it," she said.

"But I'll be whole again once we bond, I—"

"No, Rion, you won't, that's what I wanted to get across to you."

"I—" I blinked.

She wasn't going to bond with me? She didn't think I could be fixed?

What little was left of my heart began to crumble.

"Rion! Stay with me, listen to me, please." Her grip on me tightened and an urgency filled her voice.

I sucked in a breath, fighting the overwhelming loss flooding me. I could hold it together for her, for my Annie, even if only for a moment longer. I nodded as tears came again. Gods, I was such a mess.

"Rion, joining with me isn't going to make you whole. Yes, it will fill in the emptiness you feel, but your spirit is and always has been yours, not mine. I can't give you back what she took from you, from your spirit. When you join with me, you'll be exactly as you are now, but bonded. Do you understand?"

I shook my head. What was she trying to say?

Annie sighed and leaned in to kiss me lightly on the cheek. She stayed close, one hand on my face, caressing, calming. "I can't give you your spirit back," she repeated. "I can give you a bond, yes, but only that. It will fill part of what you feel is missing within you, but not all of it. I can't fill that remaining part, only you can. I needed you to know this before we bonded. I need you to understand that there will still be work you'll need to do, on you." She swallowed and sighed. "I know *she* took a lot from you. More than the others."

I nodded, my throat tight, grateful that Annie hadn't used the woman's name. The mere thought *of her* sent me to near panic.

"Some of that, I can give back," Annie went on, "but most will be up to you. You'll need to claim your power back from her. That's all I'm saying. I didn't want us to bond and have you feel like it was... incomplete. It won't be. We'll be one, together, in heart and soul. But your spirit will be up to you to reclaim."

I nodded. She was preparing me. And I understood why. I'd been going on about how lost I was, how I needed her. I did, but part of what I was feeling wasn't my need for her, but my need... for me, for what *that woman* had taken from me. "I understand."

"Good." She remained close. "Then Hyperion of the Phyllidian Forest, will you bond with me?" she pressed a finger to my lips as I was about to respond. "Not yet, there's more. I, Annie Chambers would very much like to bond with you. This would be a life bond, a commitment of your heart and soul and body to me and to the others who have bonded with me. We would be one. We would be equal, Rion. *Equal.* Each of us our own person, bringing our own strengths and abilities to this bond. Each of us helping each other in areas where we're weak. As Aethan said, we'll be stronger together, but we must be strong ourselves first. Knowing all of this, will you bond with me, Hyperion?"

She was close and I dipped in for a quick kiss, my heart filling with joy at her words. Her soft lips were responsive, eager, and I knew what she was asking.

Our first time bonding it had been so quick, so informal. She'd kissed me and I'd asked if she meant it. She hadn't even really known what she was doing then. It was very clear to me now that she was fully aware of it.

And knowing that... I had to ask myself if I was aware,

if I was ready and capable of being in this bond, with her, with the others.

I pulled away from her slightly, making her eyes widen in surprise.

"Rion?"

"I'll answer you, but can you give me a moment?"

She nodded and I rose and brought forth my wings.

"I need to fly, to think, to... remember myself," I said softly. "Can you give me the time to do that?"

She smiled as if understanding that I couldn't bond with her so emotionally unbalanced... of course that had been what she'd just told me, that our bond wouldn't fix what had been broken, that I had to find that myself.

I took off and quickly climbed high into the sky. Once there, I flared my wings out and soared, drifting so I could think.

Yes, my thoughts and feelings were still in turmoil. Yes, I was... broken... as hard as it was to admit that. I'd been helpless.

I shuddered, but forced myself to think back on the pain, the horror. My jaw tensed, clenched hard, and my body was wracked with tremors, but I forced myself to remember the pain of *her* digging out my wing.

I flinched, and fell for a second then steadied my flight.

I had my wing back.

I was whole.

I had proof. Why was it so hard to believe?

Rolling my shoulder, I flapped a bit harder, reassuring myself of that. I gained a bit of height, then set to glide once again.

She had done this.

She...

I had to say her name. If I was ever going to face her again without fear—and without a doubt Annie would want to face her and end her evil plans once and for all—I needed to be able to at least say her name.

"Hera," I choked out, that one word sickening me.

I forced myself to say it again. "Hera."

My jaw tightened and I fought a scream, then realized that was stupid and released it.

"I hate you, Hera," I snarled, tears welling in my eyes again. "You tried to take everything from me, *Hera*. You tried and you failed. I'm whole again. The pain. Is. Gone." And it was... physically. There were emotional scars still, but I knew I didn't have to face them alone.

That realization stunned me.

Against everything I'd been taught by my father, I didn't have to do it alone. Annie and the others would help me through this and it wasn't a sign of weakness.

"You failed, *Hera*." More tears leaked from my eyes even as my body still trembled at her name. Why was I afraid? Why did her name shake me? Why did the very thought of her bring me to my knees? Yes, she'd inflicted so much pain... but that was gone now. And at the time I'd thought she'd also, somehow, taken my bond with Annie, but that could be restored as well.

"I won't fear you. I won't live in your pain," I insisted.

Except there was more around that. There was the fear that I'd be captured again. The fear of more pain and suffering. The fear that she'd inflict that suffering on Annie.

If I was going to face her again, I'd need to face that fact, face that fear.

Pain was nothing new to me. My father had been a harsh man, sometimes physically so, when I'd been growing up, although the wounds he had inflicted paled in comparison with Hera's. I knew pain was fleeting, that wounds could be healed, as they had been this first time, but that did nothing to abate my fear. There was that nagging voice inside me saying, 'what if she hides you better?'

'What if you aren't found the next time?'

'What if the pain doesn't end?'

But... it would. One way or another, the pain would end. If I was captured again, I'd either die or I'd be rescued. Death might be long in coming, but it would be an end. And I didn't think that was the likely outcome anyway. Annie had rescued me once, she'd do it again. I'd never doubt her again. She'd found me the first time, and I'd thought that impossible. Now I knew. Nothing was impossible.

The pain would always end.

Annie would always come for me.

And I... I would always fight for her, and for myself. I'd fight all the harder to make sure I wasn't captured again.

Yes, I'd face Hera again, and I'd do everything in my power to repay my debt of pain to her. Did I still fear her? Yes. But I couldn't let that fear overwhelm me and endanger everyone I loved.

I smiled, a hard and cold thing.

My love for Annie and my chosen brothers was

stronger than my fear. I'd just needed to be reminded of that.

I folded in my wings and dove down to where Annie was waiting for me. I stopped my fall with a flourish, then vanished my wings and landed gently on the ground.

"I'm ready," I said, firm, decided, and I wrapped my arms around her tugging her close.

"Oh!" she said, a bit startled, as if she hadn't expected me to take charge so completely. But she leaned into my embrace and looked up at me with desire and love and confidence, giving me no doubt that she didn't mind my determination.

"I, Hyperion, no longer of the Phyllidian Forest—for you are my home now—do accept your bond, Annie Chambers. I will become one with you and with the others. One heart, one soul, one body." I shifted my hips, pressed my hard cock against her belly, and made her eyes heat with desire. "All that I have is yours, and I accept all that you are to me. Let us be so bound and committed, for now and forever."

She pulled my head down to hers and we kissed.

I felt the bond bloom within me, growing until it shook both myself and Annie, which I didn't recall happening before. This time was stronger, that much I could feel.

And in that moment, I also felt... three others warming my soul, strengthening it with their love. My brothers. They were a part of this bond as well, and I knew if any of us doubted or faltered, the other would lend strength unconditionally. I hadn't felt that before either. Truly this was a bond no one could break. Not even Hera. Let her try.

Annie drew back, breathless and shaken.

"I can feel all of you," she whispered.

"As can I," I replied.

She blinked. "Truly?"

I nodded.

She smiled, a breathtaking, sensual smile, and reached down to stroke my semi-aroused cock. "I promised you we'd 'test' out how... whole you are."

I grinned. "And we will, but I can wait for just a moment." I looked up and somehow knew I'd see the other three guys cresting the hill behind Annie. "I think we'd all like to show you exactly how we feel about you."

She raised a brow, then half turned. "Oh? Oh!" She waved her free hand for the others to join us. "Yes, I think that could work too."

CHAPTER 22

ANNIE

I COULD FEEL THEM, EACH OF MY GUYS, THEIR WARMTH inside me, wrapped around my soul. And I could feel their desire. It was glorious. They were aroused in more ways than simply physically, excited and filled with life. They wanted to celebrate the completing of our bonded group.

I closed my eyes as they drew near and drank in their love and excitement, their desire and joy. It lifted my spirits to new heights and turned me on.

We'd been together once before, all four of us, but my memory of that time was a bit fuzzy. I hadn't wanted to think at all in that moment and had just turned off my brain and enjoyed the sensations. I recalled only a few moments, Aethan's vibrating cock, hands everywhere, kneeling on Keph because I couldn't take him fully inside me... which didn't seem to be an issue anymore.

This time I wanted to remember everything, every aching, loving moment of this encounter.

As they had before, they stood close around me, and I slowly turned, taking in each of them.

Del, tall and broad, with his glistening blue-black hair falling to below his shoulders and those clear sea-green eyes shining with the warm and tender smile that brightened his face.

Aethan, swaying with anticipation, an eager grin on that ruddy face, his mane of red-brown hair bristling like a mohawk and his soft brown eyes filled with anticipation and desire.

Rion taller than Del and leaner, with stunning chiseled muscles. His long, pale-blond hair always seemed perfectly windswept and flowing, and his smile was sure and confident, his intense blue eyes taking me in as well as the others, his dearest friends.

Last, but certainly far from least, was Keph, with his mountainous frame of hard rolling muscle, from shoulders to arms and chest, abs, and legs. His onyx skin glistened as he smiled, wide and relaxed, a playful glint in his silver-rimmed, black eyes.

These were my guys. My glorious guys. Gods, how I loved them. And I was more than ready to be with them again, all as one.

"How do you want us?" Rion asked, his voice husky with desire.

Every way, all the time. Unfortunately, we weren't in my world and they didn't have their powers. Aethan couldn't vibrate and Del couldn't play with water in fun ways. Still, I knew this was going to be a moment I'd never forget.

I knelt, thinking I'd start the guys off with a little oral

teasing, but as soon as I was on my knees, I noticed a problem. We were in a field. The grasses were soft, but the myriad stones and rough earth weren't pleasant. Even if the guys were kind enough to shield me from it, it wouldn't be comfortable for them.

I rose again. "Perhaps we could go to Masia, get a room?" I offered. "It's a bit... natural here."

"If it's the little stones you're worried about, I can get rid of those," Keph said.

"You can?" Del asked, staring at Keph in surprise.

Keph nodded with a shy grin. "I probably mentioned my father is the stone-speaker of the Ophion Mountains. But I don't think I ever told you what he did."

"He speaks with stone?" Aethan asked.

"Ah... yes."

"And you can to?"

"Well, yes. In truth my father speaks to the earth itself, the mountains, the stones, the dirt and what lays below. He's much more practiced than I am. I only ever learned a little of this. But it's enough to flatten out this area and remove any offending pebbles."

We all stared at him for a long moment.

"What?" he rumbled, a bit defensively.

"Why didn't you ever tell us you could do that? Between that and your ability as a seer, you're full of surprises," Rion said.

He shrugged. "I can occasionally see the future— which has generally only gotten me in trouble—and I can move pebbles. I never thought either trait was that impressive."

No, perhaps they weren't, but still.

"Please," I said, laying a hand on his massive chest. My heart quickened just with that one bit of contact. "If you could clear out this area, I think we'd all appreciate that."

"Stand back," he said. "Things are probably going to get a bit... shaky."

Del scooped me up, holding me firm as the others braced themselves. Then the earth did shake and more violently than any of us were prepared for. Rion's wings sprouted and he took flight, hovering, while Aethan became a horse and bolted a little farther away. Del, to his credit, didn't drop me, but he did fall to one knee in the short time Keph took to do his thing.

Then it stopped.

Rion landed, and Aethan returned, flashing back into his satyr form.

"I was twenty feet away and didn't feel a thing," Aethan said in wonder.

"I just cleared this area," Keph replied, indicating a radius of perhaps five to ten feet out from where he stood.

"Amazing," Rion said as Del laid me upon the soft grasses.

"Well," my triton asked. "How is it?"

It was... I snuggled a bit into the grasses and ground. Not only was the grass lush and soft, but the earth below was free of stones and felt like it had been... tenderized. "It's lovely."

I made to rise, but then Del knelt and indicated I should just lay back. "If it's that nice, then just relax. Let's begin this with our lips upon your perfect skin." And he bent to kiss me, mid-stomach.

The others knelt as well and did the same. Keph kissed the tops of my feet, then began working his way up one leg. Rion, kneeling above my head, leaned down and kissed my forehead, then began peppering my face with kisses as well, while Aethan took up an arm and began by sucking on each of my fingers.

It was glorious and so very soothing, at least at first. Then Rion found my lips and Del sucked on my nipple and Aethan flicked the other one with his tongue and my need started to tighten into what I knew would become amazing molten desire low within me.

Keph's lips teased up my thigh, inching closer and closer to my core. He reached the crux where my legs met, oh so close to where I wanted him, but tauntingly switched to my other thigh instead.

I squirmed in my guys' grip. I didn't want him to move down the other leg, I wanted him to stay in between my thighs, using his powerful tongue to twist me tighter.

I opened my legs wider in invitation, praying he'd get the hint since Rion's lips still fully possessed mine in a powerful, demanding kiss.

Keph huffed, a low, sensual rumble and shifted, settling between my legs and sliding a hand under my ass to lift me, making it easier for him to drive me crazy with his tongue. With another low rumble, he traced my folds, drawing out the sensation then swept his tongue over my clit.

My hips jerked in anticipation and the heat inside me spun tighter. If I hadn't been fully aroused before, I was now.

But I was done being passive, so I reached out to the

sides and found Del's erection, then Aethan's. They were both hard and ready and I grasped them tightly, stroking them.

Aethan groaned, while Del drew his teeth over my nipple, spiking a flicker of delicious pain that coincided with a vigorous series of flicks by Keph's tongue. Together they sent a small rushing orgasm sweeping through me, and I gasped into Rion's mouth, sucking in his breath.

He pulled away, concern in his eyes, and check to see if I was okay.

"Enough foreplay!" I managed to gasp out and thank God they didn't need any more instruction than that.

I didn't know how they communicated, it certainly wasn't with words. Perhaps there were significant glances? Or perhaps the bond—even between them—was that close.

Del laid back, and the guys lifted me with strong and caressing hands, and helped me straddle him. I took a long moment, drawing it out for both me and Del, and eased myself onto his magnificent cock, enjoying every inch of it as I slowly took him deeper and deeper inside me.

Finally, with a shuddering breath, my desire ratchetted tight, I had him fully sheathed and could feel him throbbing within me with his rapid pulse.

Again, with a delicious torture for both of us, I started moving, grinding down as I rocked my hips, making our breaths pick up with our blossoming need.

Del cupped my breasts, caressing them, as Rion pressed a hand against my back, urging me forward so he could tease my other opening. He took a long time to fully ease past that tight ring of muscle, adding to the incredible pressure and heat building inside me, while Del kneaded and caressed my breasts and our lips mingled in a teasing, tasting dance.

I had another shuddering moment, a whisper of another climax with the promise of something amazing in my future, as Rion finally buried himself inside me, his body tucked up tight against me. Then he wrapped his arms around me and urged me to sit up, shifting where both of them rubbed inside me, hitting nerves wound tight with anticipation.

Then the guys started a slow, sensual rhythm, building a glorious heat within me.

On either side of me, Aethan and Keph watched, their eyes dark with desire, their cocks hard and erect and ready as they patiently waited their turn, Aethan a little less patiently with his hand wrapped around his cock, slowly stroking himself in anticipation.

Precum glistened on his tip, begging me to take him in my mouth, and I lifted my gaze to his, licking my lips as I reached out, and wrapped my hand around him.

He drew close and I flicked my tongue over him, making his eyes roll back in pleasure.

"Gods, you're so beautiful," Rion murmured in my ear, and I took Aethan fully into my mouth until he bumped the back of my throat, then slowly slid him out, relaxed my throat, and took him deeper.

He grunted in pleasure, his body trembling, and I worked him faster and harder, matching Rion and Del's thrusts into me.

Out of the corner of my eye, I saw Keph kneel and

press his hands to the ground. I wasn't sure what he was doing, but a few seconds later, the ground started to tremble. It wasn't as violently as before, but enough to vibrate *everything* sending rippling tremors rushing through my body and exploding into a wave of bliss.

I moaned my release around Aethan's erection, my body tensing then relaxing and flooding with more liquid heat. Del and Rion picked up the pace, Del capturing my hips and holding me steady, while Rion teased my oh-so-sensitive nipples, building on my orgasm and twisting me higher just like the other times I'd made love with them.

I took out my pleasure on Aethan, teasing and sucking and stroking, my desire making me wild. He trembled in my grip and I raised my gaze, wanting to watch him while he came.

Heat and need and love filled his soft brown eyes, rushing more heat through my body and making my soul thrum. This was right. This was the way things were supposed to be with my guys, us joined together like this in a primal dance of pleasure.

He tensed and groaned and his salty warmth rushed into my mouth. Pure pleasure filled his expression and I held him tight until he was done.

When I finally released him, he staggered back, grabbing his cock and bringing it back to full erection with little effort. I watched it rise again, shocked with how fast he recovered. But then Aethan wasn't a normal human, none of my guys were. They were magical and powerful and incredible.

Rion pulled me back a little, leaning against him, and Del ground his thumb against my clit, in slow, delicious circles. His own thrusts grew harder and faster, and my body blazed with the promise of another, more powerful orgasm.

He gave a few more, powerful thrusts, then let out a feral yell and swelled even larger, filling me completely with Rion in behind. My near-constant orgasm ramped up another level at this and I cried out with him.

He shuddered and groaned, while Rion held me still, letting us ride out our release, then, with my muscles still trembling, Rion grabbed my hips, released his wings, and lifted us off Del. He thrust long, hard strokes inside me, bringing me back up to a trembling, aching need, and brought me face to face with Keph.

I leaned forward, my lips meeting his in a devouring kiss, while Rion slowly pumped inside me, keeping me primed and thrumming.

Keph drew in closer and his massive cock brushed against me, sending another whisper of an orgasm rushing through me. I didn't know how much more my body and heart could take, but if I was going to die, I was certainly going to die happy and thoroughly satisfied.

Keph held out his large hands like a shelf, and Rion helped me settle my thighs on them, giving the large man more control of my body. He continued using his cock to tease my already well aroused and ready opening, while Rion kept thrusting in time with the slow beat of his wings.

"Soft or hard?" Keph rumbled, his stunning black, silver-rimmed eyes capturing me, body, mind, and soul.

"Hard," I gasped out. Now that I'd had him fully and knew I could take it, I didn't want him to hold back. I wanted him to have everything the others had without fear of hurting me.

He grinned and pulled me onto his cock with one powerful thrust. Once again, my body—miraculously—made room for him, although with Rion in behind, I was stretched to my limit, my pleasure verging on pain in a delicious, shuddering way. The joining of that massive cock inside me must have over-stimulated Rion, because he cried out and tensed, released in that same instant, filling me with warmth and pressure and making my muscles shudder and contract.

Oh, yes. Oh, Gods, yes.

There was something incredible about bringing these powerful men pleasure, about feeling them let go and love me, just like I was letting go and loving them.

I cried out as another wave of bliss crashed over me. Rion pinned me against Keph's hard body, their cocks buried deep inside me, as he gasped his pleasure, his body trembling. Then he carefully pulled out of me and sagged to the ground, leaving me entirely to Keph.

I wrapped my arms around his neck and met his gaze again.

"Hi," I purred.

He smiled, and thrust into me. "Hi, beautiful."

I moaned back as he thrust again, harder and faster, encouraging him because I knew he'd never been like this with a woman before, had been afraid he'd hurt his partner with his strength and size.

"Yes!" I cried, throwing my head back, trusting Keph to satisfy me, loving every powerful second I was in his arms. I'd never had sex like this before. Such a large man, so strong, so filling, thrusting deep inside me. It was every sinful fantasy I'd ever had and the look on his face, the lust and love and need, all for me, was a drug like no other.

I cried out with another release, or perhaps I'd been coming this entire time and was just reaching a new plateau, I didn't know. But with one final, incredible thrust Keph swelled and released as well.

I let out a prolonged scream of pleasure as my body convulsed, waves of bliss crashing over me, rushing through my whole body as if even my hair and toenails were hypersensitive and reacting to my orgasm.

When Keph finally set me on my feet, his arms still wrapped around me to hold me steady, I must have been a sweaty-bedraggled mess, and I didn't care. I'd had the most amazing sex with my amazing men and they all looked at me like I was the goddess they first thought I was, even though they knew I wasn't.

I found it odd that my legs weren't quivering at all. I was strong and oh-so-very fulfilled, and—holy shit!—my desire was far from quenched.

A giggle bubbled up inside me. It was like I'd become some sex goddess... or sex demon? I didn't know if that was possible. Maybe I was just so in love with these guys and my magical healing gave me incredible stamina.

Whatever it was, I wasn't going to look a gift horse in the mouth.

I glanced mischievously from Keph, to Rion, to Aethan, to Del.

"More?" I giggled.

"Truly?" Del gasped. "After Keph, I... I've never seen

him like that."

"It was incredible," I half moaned half sighed. "Let's do it again."

They didn't need to be told a third time.

Aethan was there, all furious kisses and caressing hands as he ducked and nudged his cock up to brush my opening. I lifted one leg, resting it on his hip as he adjusted his position and entered me in a smooth, powerful stroke.

Surprisingly, after having been gloriously punished by Keph's massive erection only moments ago, Aethan's much smaller cock still felt incredible. Again, somehow, I was adapting to each man as they entered me.

I wrapped my arms around him rubbing my body on his as we pressed close, undulating against each other as he thrust into me.

"I don't think any man has been ready for a second turn with me so quickly," I breathed into his ear. "You're incredible."

"I love you, Annie," he groaned back. "I'll give you whatever you want whenever you want it."

"I want you," I replied, meeting him thrust for thrust, crashing our bodies together in the most delicious way.

His pace was incredible. He didn't have super-speed in this world, but his hips were still powerful and fast. I jumped up into his arms, wrapping my legs around him as he supported my ass, and relentlessly plunged into my depths.

The bliss of an orgasm shivered through me and I grasped him tighter with my arms and legs. I was high enough that he had his head buried in my breasts and I pushed him closer still, his teeth nipping my tender skin with delicious licks of pain.

Then pressure at my other opening, drew my attention and I glanced back to see Del, close behind me. He was a bit tall to get a good angle with Aethan holding me, but he seemed to be half-crouching so he'd be able to get in.

"I want to feel all of you," he murmured, as his teasing turned to shallow penetration, and I moaned my pleasure, giving him permission.

I felt his tip first and with Aethan's unceasing rapid driving it was enough to push me over the peak of another orgasm. Apparently, that was exactly what I needed to loosen up a little and Del pushed fully inside me soon after that. His strokes were slow and long, a counterpoint to Aethan's speed, my body captured between the two of them on the precipice of another incredible orgasm.

I kept waiting for Aethan to finish, but recalled—as my body thrummed tighter and tighter—that some men lasted much longer their second time around.

Keph joined us. Raised as I was, I was nearly at a height to meet his lips. He only had to duck a little to join in with a kiss.

Rion, flew in as well, and I turned from Keph's lips to Rion's cock and grabbed it from the air to taste and pleasure.

My mind seemed to explode, overloaded with sensations, Aethan's driving need, Del's slow rocking strokes, the hard intensity of Keph's lips, and salty sweetness of Rion's cock.

Keph knelt again, the ground trembled and all the men within me were suddenly vibrating in all the right ways.

Del's strokes quickened as his erection swelled. I knew, in one glorious moment of connection, that all my guys were going to climax at once. A moment later, Aethan's final hard thrust matched Del's as they released. Rion cried out as well, filling my mouth. And for me... it was a high like I'd never experienced before, a heavenly orgasm so sweet and overpowering my muscles locked me into stillness, my release sending me spinning, lights flashing across my vision.

Eventually the moment passed. Rion landed, breathing hard, and Aethan and Del removed themselves and set me down. Like the last time, I wasn't weak or exhausted. I was empowered and strong. As they all collapsed into sweaty, exhausted heaps, I was filled with strength and drive.

It still took me some time to regain my voice, but when I did, I said, "That was the singular most amazing thing I've ever felt. Thank you. All of you."

They all smiled wearily, groaning and humming their satisfaction.

"How are you not tired?" Keph asked. He, out of all of them, seemed the least weary.

"I don't know," I giggled, my elation overwhelming me. "I'm a little baffled myself. All I know is, right now, I feel like I could take on the world."

"What about Hera?" Del asked.

I put on an eager smile. "Her, too."

CHAPTER 23

ANNIE

As the guys rested from their oh-so-amazing exertions I, feeling empowered, went to a nearby stream to wash up, then went looking for Janice. I couldn't find her on the beach, and when I asked the assembled men, a few smiled mischievous grins and pointed to the towering set of black stones where the portal was.

"She went to the other world?" I asked, suddenly concerned.

"No," Naz said, with a sheepish smile. "I believe she's just hiding on the other side of those stones. She... needed a moment to herself."

I didn't know what that meant but went to find her.

I came around to the other side of the stones to see Janice hiking up her pants. She looked flushed.

"Janice?" I asked, wondering if I was interrupting a private moment.

She jumped. "Oh, good, it's just you." Though her tone then shifted. "You little minx!"

I raised a brow at that and joined her in the small alcove of rocks where she was hiding. "Minx?"

"What were you doing?" she demanded, waggling her eyebrows suggestively at me.

"What? Oh!" I gave her a silly grin. "I was able to re-establish my bond with the guys and then we... ah... celebrated."

"Fucked like bunnies?"

Heat warmed my cheeks, although not as much as before. I wasn't ashamed of what we'd done at all. They were my mates, and I loved them. "Yep. Could you hear us?"

"Oh, there was the occasional cry from the hills, but... ah... no..." Now she was blushing, her cheeks a soft pink.

"What?" I asked.

"I could *feel* it!" she hissed. Her eyes intense and accusing.

"You could?" I asked, shocked.

Oh, shit. We were bonded. Could she feel what I felt? Would I when she found *her* someone... or someones?

"Really?" I don't know why, but I flushed even more.

"Yes!" she hissed. "Last night I kept waking up feeling really horny. I even..." Her face went from flushed to beat red. "I think I cried out in my sleep a few times and ah... well it turns out, women can have wet dreams too, it seems. I had to take a fully clothed dip in the sea this morning to cover that up. Then, just now, I... well, for a while I felt really relaxed and mellow, with a pleasant—" She cleared her throat. "Well, all the guys in camp said I had a glow about me. But then suddenly I needed very much to... ah... give myself a little release. And I wasn't about to do that in front of all those guys... especially Naz!"

"Oh." I pressed my lips together, trying not to smile or giggle. Giggling would be bad given how upset she was. It seemed my bond with Janice went so far as to share some of my feelings with her, though it sounded like the transfer was more than just emotions, but physical sensations as well. "Sorry about that."

"Yes, well, I'm... good now." She rolled her eyes and chuckled. "So what did happen out there?"

"Only the single best moment of my entire life. An orgasm so divine it defies description."

"Fuck? Really?"

"Yep," I said, actually bobbing on my toes, a silly grin on my face.

"Ah... well next time warn me when you are about to have a divine orgasm so I can find somewhere private to ah..." She cleared her throat again.

"You know, you could invite a guy along—or more than one—to help you with that," I suggested, making her cheeks red again. "Maybe Naz?"

"I'm not at that point with Naz, yet."

"Oh? I'm sure all you'd have to do is ask and he'd be there for you."

"Well, I'm not ready to ask," she insisted, but her tone said she was seriously considering it.

I shrugged. "Your call."

She straightened. "Now I should probably get back out there before those guys think something strange is happening between us."

I hated to tell her, but— "I think they already think

something is happening. The few who saw you leave were all a bit... odd about it," I chuckled.

"Fuck, not Naz?"

"Yeah, him too."

"Ah, fuck! I'll never be able to look at him without blushing ever again!"

I put an arm around her shoulders and accompanied her as she walked around the rocks and headed back to camp. "Don't worry, you look lovely when you blush, I'm sure he won't mind at all."

She elbowed me in the ribs... hard.

I grunted, tears coming to my eyes half in pain and half in mirth. "Ow."

"You're a healer," she huffed. "Heal."

I blinked the tears away. "Yeah, I guess I deserved that. So, anyway, to the real reason I came to find you. I'm feeling like I want to go after Hera again. At the moment, I know we can defeat her, but I'm curious what you think on the matter."

"We have the same resources we did last time," Janice said, as we headed toward the surf, away from the camp, in part to discuss our options and also to avoid the guys who might be curious about what happened to Janice. "And she'd be ready for us."

Which was something I feared and the reason I'd asked Janice for her thoughts on the matter, hoping she'd have a solution to the problem.

"We have to assume she isn't just waiting in her penthouse. She knows we can teleport in and out now. She'll have moved to someplace secret and safe. And—and this is a big one—she probably still has the portal staked out.

Anyone who walks through there, is gonna get shot up really darn quickly."

Right.

Fuck.

"There's no other portal that you know of?" she asked.

I shook my head. "Not that I know of."

I thought about that, a whirlwind of questions rushing through my mind.

"Here's a question," I said, thinking out loud. "Hera should be able to use the portal, so why hasn't she come through with her goons and squashed us?"

"That's a horrifying thought. But... you're right," Janice replied. "Why hasn't she? With the forces she has at her command—and those she could buy—she'd have no trouble wiping this world clean. Assuming guns worked here. Have we tested that?"

"No, I've never had a gun with me."

"I do," Janice said. She pulled out her handgun and fired a quick shot down into the sand, proving it worked well enough.

I jumped a little at the roar as it went off even though I'd expected it.

Janice holstered her weapon. "I don't get it. Some of these folks can fly or turn into animals, but they don't have the amazing powers they have on the other side, so why not face them here?"

"Maybe she can't?" I said, although it was more of a question than a statement, and I had no idea why she wouldn't be able to.

Janice raised a brow at that.

My mind spun faster and faster. Perhaps it was the amazing sex which had cleared the cobwebs, but I felt like I was quicker, more lucid. Hera should have come through by now. She'd have the advantage of numbers and superior weapons here. There was no reason for her not to come and wipe us all out... unless she couldn't.

And, the last time we'd gone back, there had been that strange man—one of her agents—waiting for us, for me. She'd wanted me to go to her, as if there was something I had which she didn't.

Except I couldn't figure out what that could be. She had everything, including stronger powers than me, but if she'd lost her ability to cross between worlds, then that would be something I could do that she couldn't.

"I think Hera's lost her ability to cross between worlds," I said. The more I mulled it over, the more it made sense. "If she could, she'd be here. She has all the advantages here, assuming she brings her small army with her. It also explains why she wanted me to surrender myself. There isn't anything I have that she doesn't have, except maybe that."

Janice nodded. "Well, let's be thankful for that then, otherwise we'd probably all be dead by now."

I nodded, grateful indeed.

"But still," Janice said. "Assuming she doesn't care about that anymore, anyone who goes through that portal, even potentially you, is dead."

"Except you," I said, realizing it as I said it.

"Me?"

"You went through, got shot several times, and weren't hurt."

"That was... I don't know what that was." She frowned, her expression a mix of fear and uncertainty.

"It must be your superpower."

"But I'm not bulletproof. I've been shot before."

Right. Perhaps we could try a different approach to figuring that out. "Assuming you do have some sort of superpower, you've probably had it your entire life, since you've always had *aurai* blood in you. Is there anything you can do better than others, like, a lot better?"

Janice gave a quick laugh. "Drink."

I didn't see how that was a power, but it could be a clue to something else. "Tell me about that."

She shrugged. "I started drinking young. My dad thought everyone should get a taste for alcohol early. It would either dissuade them or prepare them. For me, well, I sort of liked it. I come from a larger family, one younger sister and four brothers, only one of whom is younger. My sister was the girly-girl, not me. I was more like my brothers, rough and tumble. I drank like they did, even though I was half their size." She gave another laugh. "The first time I tried to match them drink for drink, oh God, was I sick, it was nasty! But after that, I kept up with them just fine, in fact I began to be able to outdrink them, usually with little or no side effects." She frowned and cocked her head to one side. "Hunh, now that I say it, that does seem fairly extraordinary. Perhaps that's my power?"

"Incredible drinking ability?" Maybe, but I knew she'd been shot and somehow come away unscathed and had a strong suspicion there was more to it. "Anything else?"

We walked in silence for a long moment before she said, "Sleep."

"You think your super power is sleep?"

"No, not sleep, but being able to go without it."

"Go on," I prompted.

She made a bit of a face, as if more and more of what she was saying—what she'd probably taken for granted —now seemed... odd when analyzed.

"It's sort of the same story. In university, I studied hard, like really hard. I stayed up for three days straight once and then crashed, just before an exam actually. But ever since then, I haven't had any problems going a day or two without sleep. I hardly notice it. I can stay out drinking all night and still feel refreshed in the morning even when the FBI guys I was drinking with were all bleary-eyed and half dead."

"That sounds less like a power around drinking and sleeping, and more something to do with fortitude or stamina."

"Yeah, it does, doesn't it?"

"And maybe that transfers to being shot as well." My clearer-than-ever mind was starting to work once again.

Janice raised a brow at me, skeptical.

"No, listen." Words tumbled out as I thought this through. "You had a bad drinking experience, then after that, you were an amazing drinker. You had a bad sleeping experience, then you were okay without sleep. You got shot once, and now, maybe you can't get shot again?" Before she could refute this, I asked, "Has there been anything else in your life that went badly once, but has been great since?"

She opened her mouth, then closed it, thinking. After a moment she said, "Well, yeah, sort of."

"And?"

She quirked her mouth. "Well I'd thought it was just because I was in top physical condition, but this matches what you're saying." She sighed heavily. "When I was training for the PFT, I—"

"PFT?" I asked.

"Sorry, the FBI Physical Fitness Test. PFT."

"Ah, okay."

"Anyway, when I was training for the running portion, I wanted to really challenge myself so I borrowed all the gear from a firefighter friend of mine. I suited up with all fifty pounds of it, then for good measure added a few ankle and wrist weights and set off on my run." She grinned. "I finished the one-and-a-half-mile run, but then collapsed and blacked out. Luckily, I had a friend there and they got me to a hospital. I nearly died from heat stroke and extreme exhaustion. It took me days to recover, but I was stubborn and determined to try it again. The next time, I was a bit more careful, but the second time was a breeze. I hardly felt tired at the end. And when I ran the course for real, without all the gear, I did it in record time."

She looked at me, but I didn't reply. It seemed so obvious to me, but I had a feeling she needed to say it to really believe it.

She huffed. "Yeah, okay, it seems you're right. I guess, I just... adapt well, to... anything and everything. Even apparently being shot."

The way Janice said it, sparked something for me.

This last sex-capade with the guys, I'd seemed to be a perfect fit for all of them, even massive Keph, who I'd never been able to take in fully before. But now I could adapt to his size then to Aethan and the others. If Janice had my abilities, perhaps I'd gained hers as well. It seemed logical.

But I wanted to confirm that was what Janice's power was.

"There is a way to test our theory," I said with a shrug. "You do have a gun with you. I can heal you if it doesn't work. Actually, you have my powers now too, so you can even heal yourself."

She looked at me like I had two heads. "Shoot myself?"

"Someplace non-vital. Only if you want to be sure." I shrugged.

"Fuck." But she took out her gun and grimaced at me. "This is a terrible idea."

"But the only way to know for sure." I didn't like the idea of her shooting herself, either, but we needed cold, hard—possibly painful—evidence.

"Fine." She removed her pants, sat, and aimed for the fleshy part of her thigh. Her breath picked up and her hands trembled, and she sucked in big breath after big breath.

Then, with a scream, she pulled the trigger.

The weapon roared to life and she screamed in agony, but she didn't gush blood. She didn't even weep blood. There was no wound at all and we had no idea where the bullet had gone.

For a second I wondered if she'd missed, but tears

leaked down her cheeks and she panted, confirming she'd been hurt.

"Fuck fuck fuck," she hissed. "Fuuuuuuck! That hurt."

"But you're not bleeding."

She stared at her leg. "I'm not."

"That's got to be your superpower," I said. "You're adaptable."

"Well... fuck me," Janice groaned.

CHAPTER 24

AETHAN

"I don't like it," Naz said, shaking his head. "I don't care if you're immune to their weapons, you'll still be in danger." He looked at Janice with all the intensity of devotion that I and the others looked at Annie.

A small group of us had gathered to discuss our plan for going back to the other world. Annie and all of us bonded to her were there, as was Janice, Naz, Khyrys the female minotaur who could read minds, Rhou the *panai* who could look like anything or anyone, and Dorios the *oreadai* who could— what was the word Annie used? *Teleport*.

The first part of the plan was simple. Janice would go through and distract or fight the men waiting in the alley, since she couldn't be hurt by their weapons. Keph would be in the front line as well since bullets pretty much bounced off him.

The next part was me.

"She only has to distract them for a moment," I said. "Just long enough for me to get through and start running. Once up to speed, I'm sure they won't be able to hit me and I can snatch away all their weapons. Between the three of us, we should have them dealt with quickly."

Naz still didn't look happy. He didn't want to go back at all. I wasn't sure what his power was, but whatever it was, it made him sick with a pounding headache.

"Fine," he huffed, his expression turning resigned as he realized he wasn't going to convince Janice not to do this.

In my mind the real problem wasn't dealing with the 'gate guards' so much as finding and dealing with Hera. Annie seemed upbeat and positive about our chances, but I wasn't sure why.

"Once we're safely on the other side," Annie continued, "Khyrys and I will see if we can get information from any of Hera's 'gate guards'. That will determine our next move. If she's at her building, then Dorios will teleport a small group of us to see if Del or I can sense Hera using our water sense. We've been close enough to her now that hopefully we can identify her."

Del nodded. He didn't look certain though. He said he didn't have a great range with his abilities, and he wasn't able to practice in our world where he didn't have them. Again, though, Annie was hopeful.

"If she's not there, we'll regroup at the safe house and plan from there," Annie said. "Wherever she is, everyone focus on her guards. I'll be the one to deal with her."

Annie hadn't said how she was dealing with Hera yet, only that she had an idea. I would have liked more information or more than just 'an idea,' given what had happened the last time, but that's all she'd given us.

There were serious faces all around, including Annie's. Everyone knew this was dangerous.

"There is still the matter of payment," Khyrys said, her voice gruff.

"My offer still stands," Annie replied. "You can loot whatever you want from Hera's house."

"That didn't happen last time," Khyrys shot back.

"This time we're dealing with her for good. I'll make sure you get your chance to take what you wish."

Khyrys frowned, but didn't press the issue.

"Are we set then?" Janice asked.

Everyone nodded and the group broke up to settle in for the night.

One night's sleep and then we'd go back to Annie's world. The idea made my stomach hurt and my heart pound. I didn't want Annie going back. I didn't want to risk Hera getting her hands on her.

"Annie," I said, jerking my chin, indicating I wanted to talk to her. Just her and the other guys.

She nodded and we stepped away from Janice, Naz, and Khyrys.

"What's this idea you have?" Rion asked her, before I could. "We need to know. I want to face Hera again and repay my debt of pain, but she's powerful. I— *We* can't risk you."

She wrapped her hands around his biceps and drew him close as we wandered back to our little private camp just beyond the beach.

"It's still only half formed," she replied, then held up a hand before the rest of us could argue with her. "I know that's not reassuring, but I just know that we can beat her this time." She looked at each of us in turn. "This new bond is different from the last. It's stronger. The way I feel all of you is incredible."

I couldn't disagree with that. Before I'd had a good connection with Annie, but now it was incredibly close. I could feel her confidence and calm, and beyond that, I could feel a connection with the other guys as well. It was hard to explain, but I just *knew* things about them. A simple look conveyed so much now. It was... intense. Annie was right about that much.

"My idea... well, it... I need to get close to Hera, touch her. There was something that passed between us the last time when she touched me and broke our first bond. I... don't think this new bond will break so easily. But I think when I was connected with her, that I took her ability to open portals. I can't be certain about that, but I know... something went from her to me while we were connected and I was trying to fight her. The more I think about it, the more I believe that's what happened. And if I can take that... I think— No, I *know* I can take more. She said she could take the magic from her bonds. I think I can take her magic from her. It'll be a battle of wills between us but I know with the strength of our bond coursing through me I can defeat her."

A battle of wills.

With an ancient goddess.

It was crazy. And yet, Annie felt different to me now. Powerful. Supported by the four of us.

"I know you can do it," I said and the others nodded and grunted their acknowledgement as well. Keph was firm, reassuring, like me. Del was less so, but willing to go along with the plan. Rion was the least convinced, but he nodded, and Annie invited him for a 'walk' to help calm his nerves.

I was half asleep when they returned. Rion seemed stronger, more confident, and Annie was glowing with life and energy. I don't know if they'd talked, but I was certain there had been more than just walking happening. I smiled, glad Rion was on board, and fell into a peaceful sleep.

Annie woke me early with dawn only a smudge of light on the horizon.

"Come with me," she said.

I did, rising quickly. "What is it?" I asked, although I had a strong suspicion what she desired.

"I always feel stronger and braver, more confident after I've been with one of you," she said softly, confirming my suspicion. "Today is a big day. I want to have a moment with each of you to make sure I'm on my game."

I was more than happy to go with her. Once we were far enough away, she turned to me, pressing close and capturing my lips in a long, passionate kiss.

"I liked the way you did it the last time we were alone," she murmured against my lips before turning and pressing her behind against me, my hard cock between her cheeks.

I obliged her, pushing into her tight, slick, warmth, drawing a throaty moan of satisfaction, then driving her to gasping, moaning heights of pleasure.

The coupling was quick, but thoroughly satisfying, filling me with strength and energy and certainty.

"Now I'm ready," she said, through heavy breaths, grinning at me.

I escorted her back to the camp, where she woke and left with Rion. I winked at him as he left, then I began preparing a meal.

The others woke and had their time with Annie, returning to a large meal of fruit and roasted meat, and I could feel certainty and vitality radiating from all of us.

We joined Janice and the others at the portal. Everyone looked nervous, but Annie and Janice's confidence was contagious. We may have been worried, but we were also determined.

Hera needed to be stopped and whether we wanted to be or not, we were the ones best suited to stop her.

With a quick nod from Annie, Janice stepped through the portal then Keph followed a moment later.

I counted down slowly from ten, then drew in a long breath, and stepped through.

The frozen Chicago air slapped me in the face, but I leaped into action, taking in the scene as I ramped up my speed. Keph and Janice were moving toward the mouth of the alley, both moving as fast as they could toward the men with guns firing at them. Neither was moving fast. Keph was slow to begin with and Janice seemed to be in pain from all the shots she was taking.

A bullet zipped past my head.

I gritted my teeth and pushed myself to move faster. Suddenly everyone was moving in slow motion. Even the bullets slowed to a speed where I could see them coming and avoid them.

I reached the guards at the end of the alley before

either Keph or Janice. Plucking their weapons from the hands of the guards, a couple at a time, I ran back to place them where Keph was about to step so he'd crush them.

There were a dozen men there, and in an instant, they were harmless.

Then I sped away, running to disarm the other men stationed farther away, in buildings or on roofs.

The fight was over quickly, as Annie had anticipated, and we rounded up Hera's men and identified a leader among them. Once all our troops were through the portal, Annie and Khyrys went to interrogate the leader to learn where Hera was hiding.

"Where is Hera?" Annie asked pleasantly. "Or June Olympios as she might be known to you."

"I'll never tell you, bitch!" the man spat.

Khyrys turned and nodded to Annie, indicating that the minotaur had read the man's mind and gotten useful information.

"How many guards are around her?" Annie asked.

"Go to hell!"

Khyrys nodded again.

"When is she the most vulnerable or have the least guards?"

"Fuck you!"

Khyrys snorted and rolled her eyes, trying not to laugh.

"Anything else helpful we should know?"

The man grinned and Khyrys shrugged. Guess there wasn't much more they could learn. Two tritons marched the man over with the others, while Khyrys reported to the rest of us what she'd learned.

"Hera is in a house, outside the city," the minotaur said. "From the picture in the man's mind, it's a vast house. There are over a hundred guards in and around the place. There's a lot of open land around the house as well, and we'll be seen approaching it. It'll be difficult to get past them. According to the man's thoughts, he believes she's most vulnerable when she goes for a run. She only takes a few guards with her and there are times when she may be far removed from the guards at the house, but she will also be somewhere on the vast property, perhaps hard to find. As for helpful information, I got only a strange word: pump-er-nickel?"

"It could be a pass phrase of some sort," Janice said. With that, Dorios teleported us to Janice's safe house in small groups to plan for the next phase of the mission.

This was it. We were going to get another chance to end Hera, and this time, I wasn't going to go down easily.

THE FIRST PART OF THE PLAN WENT OFF WITHOUT ANY issues and we'd regrouped in a house that Janice referred to as a safe house. Then Janice and Dorios—disguised in the armor we'd taken from Hera's 'gate guards'—along with Rhou—who could disguise himself with his magic —went back to the alley and took one of the large cars used by Hera's guards. They drove to Hera's estate to scout out the location, get a better idea of the layout of the house and grounds, and check out where Hera did her running, in preparation for our attack the next day.

Even though we knew Hera might become suspicious if her guards didn't check in during the day, we didn't want to rush the attack. Better to have more information and be prepared than not enough.

The next morning, Annie once again had a moment with each of us. I was last, and by the time she got to me, she was already radiant. I'd felt the incredible arousal of each of the other men before me through our bond and was more than ready when she climbed up into my arms.

It was also wonderful to know that I didn't need to be slow and careful with her—which still astounded me. I could just let go and enjoy the moment with her.

Once everyone was ready, Dorios started teleporting us in small groups to Hera's estate.

He moved me and the other guys, along with Annie, into a forested glade, and then Aethan was off in a flash, scouting the area. Janice and Rhou were already there in their stolen armor, looking like Hera's soldiers, while the others had been ferried into other parts of the forest, spreading us out to make our attack.

It wasn't long before the soft pounding of running foot falls started coming closer and everyone tensed, ready to make our strike.

Hera was supposed to have six men with her on her run, but when the troop came into view, there were many more than that. A full dozen ran ahead of her, a line of six ran to either side of her, and another dozen came after. There were thirty-six, where there should have been six, but given that Hera probably suspected something was up, the extra guards weren't surprising.

Everyone tensed but we wouldn't call off the attack. We'd already established we would go ahead no matter any changes. The plan was essentially the same. The only thing that could have thrown us off was if Hera had decided not to go for her regular run. But both Annie and Janice figured Hera was too cocky to do that. And they'd been right.

One of the *epimelidai* in our group turned into living fire and charged into the guards at the front of Hera's party.

The guards yelled out, some screamed, and rushed to face the attack, but Aethan zipped in stealing their guns, while Del concentrated on 'stealing people's water,' and Rion blinded them with his light. I leaped in, rushing toward a group near Hera, determined to take out as many as I could, as fast as I could.

A rapid crack-crack-crack erupted through the yells, and my chest stung, telling me one of them had gotten some shots off. The bullets hurt like Hades—these guns must have been more powerful than the ones used before —but they still didn't do a lot of damage to me, and I pushed on, barreling through the group, shoving them into each other and bowling some of them over. I rammed my fist into one man's face, sending him flying, then kicked another. He screamed and crumpled to the ground.

Chaos rang all around. Men screamed, some in pain, others calling orders. Shots roared around me, and through it all, Hera laughed. She stood in the center of it all, her head thrown back, laughing as if our attack was the funniest thing in the world.

I spun on her, slamming my fist toward her face. But she borrowed my strength, easily caught my hand, and threw me back over her head like I was a ragdoll.

I crashed through the trees, landing hard, but that hardly hindered me, and I was up a moment later, charging back in.

Fewer and fewer of the enemies had *guns* as Aethan did his job, and I tackled three more men, taking them to the ground as I reached the group on the other side of Hera.

But she wasn't looking at me anymore. She was staring down Annie, who'd moved with incredible speed to get up next to her.

This was what we'd planned. Annie just needed to touch Hera, engage with her and...

Crack-crack-crack.

Dark blood blossomed on Annie's chest as the three shots tore through her. Her eyes widened with shock and pain, and she dropped to the ground, her body suddenly limp.

I screamed, along with the others, as agony tore through me. I could feel what she felt and it staggered me, bringing me to my knees.

I wanted to go to her, *had* to go to her, but I was too slow. Time stuttered and stretched as I tried to rise and run to her.

I felt so weak. Perhaps this was the downside of this greater bond we shared.

And the question that hung in my mind as I stumbled toward the woman I loved was simple: if she died, would I?

And if I didn't, would I want to?

CHAPTER 26

THE BULLETS TORE INTO ME, ONE JUST UNDER MY LEFT breast, another near the center of my chest, and the last high on my right side, near my shoulder, then I dropped to the ground

Except there was no pain, just stillness, my body too numb with shock for my brain to register what had happened. My warmth rushed out of me and a soul-numbing cold threatened to consume me.

Not that far away, on the other side of Hera who howled with laughter, Keph staggered. He seemed so weak and awkward as he tried to rise and stumble forward. I saw this, but didn't really know what it meant. My mind was muddled, hazy, my senses growing dim. What had been sharp sounds and scents a moment before were now dull.

I was sure I knew what was going on. I'd just thought about it, thought about—

I coughed and tasted the metallic tang of blood on my tongue. That didn't seem like it was a good thing.

Darkness swam across my vision and my soul drew further and further back from everything as if I was shrinking... or being yanked away or...

I didn't know.

I was cold and getting colder.

The world grew dimmer, the darkness swelling, consuming all thought, all feeling, all—

"No!" The voice was distant and it sounded odd, like a mixture of voices all at once, and oddly, one of them sounded like mine. "Get up Annie! Heal yourself!"

Heal...

Myself...?

But I wasn't in pain. Why did I need healing? Here in this darkness, everything was serene... and empty. I didn't need healing. There wasn't anything left of me, no body, no thought.

No body...

I was sure I'd had one before... hadn't I? I couldn't remember. Was that a good thing or a bad thing?

It was so peaceful here, but so... empty. I was missing something, something important, something I didn't want to live without...

My guys. My guys were gone.

My soul lurched at that.

No—

They weren't gone. Hera hadn't taken them again, they were just too far away... no *I* was too far away. Then four faintly glowing shapes appeared in the darkness. One small and lithe with weird looking legs that ended in hooves. One massive, a giant of a man in all proportions. One broad and strong but with the tail of a fish. And one tall and lean with chiseled features and wings.

Did I know them?

"Annie!" they called. And again, my voice seemed to call with them.

They seemed to know me. They were... I *knew* who they were. I did. I just couldn't find that knowledge in the darkness.

"Yes?" I responded... only I didn't. I didn't speak, I didn't have energy or breath. I was sure I'd spoken and yet I hadn't.

Of course not, said some distant part of my mind. *You can't speak without a mouth, without a body.*

That made sense.

"I've lost my body," I said to the glowing figures, realizing as I did, that once again I wasn't actually saying anything.

"Come back to us, Annie!" the figures called.

Back?

Back where?

They certainly seemed insistent. I had to know them, and I was more and more certain that I was indeed this 'Annie' they were talking to.

"Do I..." I stopped myself this time. I'd been about to ask if I knew their names. I felt like I should. It was on the tip of my... except, I didn't have a tongue right now.

Names...

The figures were reaching out for me and I felt... love? Yes, love. It was so intense it radiated like the light around them, growing stronger and brighter and warmer.

One of them brushed the cheek I no longer had, caressing my soul and in an instant I knew.

Hyperion. Rion. A winged man. An Angel. A man of light. A man I loved deeper and more binding than anything else in the world.

Another brush of light. Aethan. Fast and lithe. A vigorous and eager lover. And I loved him just as much as I loved Rion.

I reached out to the last two, connecting with Delphon, at home in the waters. Broad and strong and loyal. And Kephas. A giant with a tender soul. Hard body. Stronger than anything or anyone, yet gentle and kind.

Together, with the others, they were mine. My guys. I loved them all and they loved me.

I felt their pull, their desire and hope and longing. I didn't know what I was being pulled toward, but I desperately wanted... needed to go to them.

I blurred into their light, joining with them, became one shining beacon. Then... I was slammed back into screaming agony.

Back into my damaged body.

I had so little energy left, I was weak, and fragile, and dying. But I knew I could heal this. I could fix these wounds. And even though I was so very low on life, I was being fed power from my guys, my loves, my bonded.

I grasped my healing power and shoved it into my wounds, slowly returning to myself, my mind clearing, my breath steadying. And it was only then that I realized I hadn't been breathing. I'd been dead.

I sucked in a long, gasping breath, and the laughter nearby stopped suddenly.

Hera.

I grinned a manic, furious grin, and opened my eyes. My guys were all feeding me so much power, I felt like I floated to my feet— No I *was* floating, using Del's water power to lift myself.

I didn't know what look was in my eyes in that moment, but Hera's eyes went wide with shock.

She scooped up a nearby gun with her wind powers, setting it in her waiting hand then pointing it at me, and fired.

Agony slammed into my head, and I slapped my palms over the point of impact.

"Fuck! That hurt!" I snarled, then realized I wasn't bleeding and I sure as hell wasn't dead.

Well, shit. I'd been right. Janice had shared her adaptation powers with me when we'd bonded and now that I'd been shot once, I couldn't be harmed again.

A manic giggle escaped my lips. I hadn't really wanted to test that theory. It had been far too dangerous since I'd almost died, but hell. I'd been right!

Hera's eyes widened even farther, and I stepped toward her, moving with Aethan's speed.

One minute I was a few feet away, the next I was right beside her.

"Come to me," I said, laying a hand on her cheek.

"How...?" she gasped.

I dipped forward and kissed her. She stiffened and I captured her head in my hands. I couldn't let her get away. I had to finish this now.

She screamed and clawed at my wrists, her grip enhanced with Keph's power.

But I had Keph's power, too, and I clung to her, bonded with her, and then pushed through her resistance somehow on instinct, and sucked out her powers, just like she'd sucked out the powers of her bonded so long ago.

I had no idea how I was doing it, how it had come so easily to me when I thought I'd have to struggle to succeed at this part of the plan, but I wasn't going to question it. My guys were with me, feeding me their life and power, and right now... I could do anything!

She heaved and writhed, clawing and punching, screaming into my mouth as I took everything from her.

Then a matching pressure swelled inside me, as she desperately clawed at my power, trying to take mine away from me. The bond went two ways and she was strong.

But I had something she didn't. Hera had never truly cherished her bonded. She'd used them for their powers, nothing more. And when she'd drained them, she'd taken their powers, but she'd also lost something. Her connection to them. She'd lost the strength that came from that bond, but I hadn't. I was stronger. Five times stronger. And I had the force of will and power of five hearts and souls behind me.

Strength from Keph.

Vigor from Aethan.

Water from Del, to physically drain her, weaken her.

And Rion's light to overwhelm her with its purity.

Even my bond with Janice, allowing me to adapt, made me stronger.

Hera gasped and moaned, her body weakening, and I could feel through our bond that she now knew her mistake. She'd tried to take my bonds, tortured my guys, tried to take everything from me, and hadn't finished the job. She should have made sure I was dead, because I'd come back stronger and now it was my turn to take everything from her and end this.

I pulled my lips away, taking the last of her power with me and felt a thousand feet tall as I released Hera.

She stumbled back, emaciated and weak, her eyes wild.

"It's not possible," she gasped as she sagged to her knees. "I'm the only one who can take powers. How could you...?"

"I still have friends and lovers." I knelt beside her. "I don't want them just for their powers. I want them for everything they are and that bond makes me stronger."

"No," she gasped again.

"Yes." I still didn't know exactly how I'd taken her powers. Yes, I'd bonded with her, but there was no love there. It had been a brutal and forced thing—probably what she'd done with her bonded, and now she knew what it felt like.

I rose and glared down at her.

"Now you have nothing. Your immortality is gone and you'll soon wither and die." I didn't know if that was true, but even if she didn't, she still only had an average human life left.

She sneered. "I'm still the richest and most powerful woman in the world! There won't be any place you can go where I can't find you and when I do, I'll—"

A shot rang out and Hera jerked back, her eyes wide and empty.

I blinked as Janice stepped into sight holding her gun, her expression hard with determination. "She was right. We couldn't let her live. She'd escape any justice we tried to put her through. She was too powerful, to wealthy."

I stared at Janice unable to fully comprehend what had happened.

It was over.

Just like that.

Janice had killed Hera.

"You..." I murmured.

"Did what had to be done," Janice replied, "something I knew you wouldn't. Your heart is too good."

I glanced back at Hera, her expression blank, her body already starting to shrivel with her impossible age.

Janice may be right, but still...

I shoved that thought aside. It was done now and there wasn't a chance Hera would return. Janice had done what Hera should have done to me and hadn't. Finished it for good.

"Thank you," I said, although my voice was hollow. As much as she may have been right, I still couldn't shake how horrible I felt that I was responsible for Hera's murder.

Then strong arms wrapped around me, four sets in a massive group hug, and I folded into my guys, melted into their love, as Janice turned and walked away.

It was done.

Finally done.

CHAPTER 27

THE FEW REMAINING GUARDS SPREAD THE WORD TO THE rest of those on the estate. By the time we got to the main house, it was empty, and already partially looted. Some of the mercenaries from the other world began to pick the place clean, but both Janice and I suspected Hera wouldn't keep her most valuable items out in the open. We went on a bit of a treasure hunt with Ladon, the triton who could sense through walls, and soon enough, in Hera's massive office, we found a secret room. We searched a bit for the hidden mechanism that would move the bookcase out of the way, but we didn't want to waste too much time in case someone had alerted the authorities, so Keph just smashed through the wall for us.

On the other side was... I didn't have the words to express the amount of wealth displayed in the large room. We each selected a few prized items, most of which were inlaid with gems or made of gold, then we stuffed our pockets with some of the smaller, more portable loot. After that, the surviving mercenaries finished cleaning it up for us. Several had died in the fight, including Khyrys the minotaur and all but one of her crew, which made my chest hurt just thinking about it. So many had died for our cause and there wasn't any way I could repay them for their sacrifice.

By the time we left, Hera's house was picked clean.

Then Janice called in the FBI to take charge of the scene and by the time they got there, the rest of us were long gone.

I moved to Eytheron, and the guys and I built a house just back from the beach near the rocks and the portal. It was fairly simple in design, many square rooms, as part of a larger square around a central courtyard. There were six bedrooms, two bathing rooms, and the southern side of the house was an open concept kitchen, dining, and living area, with no outer walls, just a spectacular view of the sea.

We each had our own room with a bed and a chest of drawers for our few items—since clothes weren't a thing, and my room had a particularly large and sturdy bed, since it needed to be able to hold all of us.

The house had gone up quickly, in roughly two weeks. The villagers from Masia had helped, supplying some materials, food, and labor. They'd been a little disappointed that we hadn't built in the village, but we were close enough they could make the trek out if they ever did need the miracle healing of 'Anichambers' as they called me.

That was another major shift in my life. My dream, since leaving university, had been to be a virtual assistant, living on a beach.

Well, I had the beach part, but the virtual assistant part was impossible in this world.

I suppose I could have made it work, returning to my world for jobs, but... when I'd started trying to set that up, I realized I didn't want that anymore. I had a much more hands-on way of helping people now, as a healer. And I loved it. People came from Masia—and all the surrounding lands—for help with things as simple as cuts and bruises, to much more serious and severe issues like complicated child-birth and deadly illnesses. Some people came to me who'd been crippled for years.

It was hard some days, seeing the pain and suffering of people, but then... they were always so happy and joyous when they left and that made it all worth it.

During that time, I also went back and forth to Chicago a fair bit. There were many things I'd needed to tend to, like giving my notice for my apartment and taking what I'd wanted from it.

Which had been an odd moving party, lugging my furniture down the street and into an alley... where it vanished!

We got lots of strange looks from passersby, but I didn't care. I was moving to paradise with the men I loved.

I'd put my financial situation in order and visited my old job, explaining that I'd had some harrowing life circumstances that I didn't want to talk about and wasn't coming back. I'd hugged Diane and wished her well, saying I was moving to the tropics like I always wanted and would be out of contact for a while.

Most of the loot I'd taken from Hera's place I'd given

to charity. I hadn't felt right keeping it. It felt like blood-money. Some had gone to paying off my credit card debt —which I'd only racked up because of Hera, but the rest went to charity. Once my cards were paid off, I cut them up and withdrew what little remained in my bank accounts. I bought myself a couple nice items to take to the other world—or to wear if and when I returned to this one—and that was it. I had nothing, no "earthly" wealth... and I was just fine with that.

The final step was the hardest and I put it off for six weeks hoping I'd figure out the right way to do it. I had no idea what to tell my family, but I couldn't just disappear on them. That would be cruel and while they didn't understand me, I still loved them.

Now, six weeks later with spring having returned to Chicago, I stood in the alley with my whole family—my father, brother, and sister—my stomach churning with uncertainty because I had no idea what to say to them and this wasn't a conversation we could have over the phone.

No one would believe me if I just told them. They needed proof.

"Why are we in an alley?" Sheri asked, her tone hesitant and worried, something I couldn't blame her for because we *were* in an alley.

I considered saying, 'I live here now,' but that seemed like a cruel joke. Instead I said, "I have something I wanted to tell you all. But I knew if I just told you, you'd think I was crazy and lock me in an asylum somewhere. So, I thought I'd show you."

"Show us what?" Sheri's frown deepened.

"This," I said and I walked through the portal. To them it would look like I just walked through a brick wall, so I returned almost instantly before one of them had a breakdown.

Three stunned set of eyes stared at me.

"See, crazy, hunh?" I said, trying to keep the situation light.

"Wha...?" my father tried.

"Did you want to try? I promise it won't hurt." I took my father's hand and led him through the portal. He shied away from the wall as I pulled him closer, but I had Keph's strength now and I easily tugged him through.

He blinked at the shining sun in the other world and the brilliant blue sky.

"Wha...?" he repeated. "Where...?"

I laughed and said, "I'll be back in a moment, I'm going to go get the others."

I led them through one by one, each of them stunned at the sunny beach, a mix of shock and wonder filling their expressions.

"Welcome to Eytheron, the Okanid Islands." I threw out my arms to indicate the world around us.

"Those names don't mean anything," my father said, the first to recover—probably because he'd been staring at his surroundings the longest. "Where are we?"

"On another world," I said grinning. "This is where I live now."

"L-live?" my brother stammered, his body shaking with what was starting to look like serious shock.

"Yep. Isn't it nice?" I pointed to the large, squat structure nearby. "That's my home."

They all looked. Then several of their eyes went wide.

My sister gasped. "Oh!"

I looked, thinking I knew what they were seeing and... yup, there was Keph and Del, standing in the open-sided living area completely naked.

A man-shaped shadow passed over us and I sighed. Apparently, the guys had decided to ignore my suggestion that they stay hidden for the first part of this, until I'd gotten around to explaining them to my family.

Rion landed with a flap of his white wings and all eyes turned to him. At least he was wearing the leather wrap-skirt he'd had on when we'd first met.

"An angel!" Sheri gasped.

"Hello, my name is Hyperion. But for Annie's family, you can call me Rion." He held out a hand as I'd shown him. My father shook it, but I think that was more on instinct than actual acceptance.

"Are you..." my sister began, whispering to me. "Is he... your... he's gorgeous!"

I grinned and waggled my eyebrows at her unable to help myself. Yes. He was.

"So, ah, yeah," I said. "I now live on another world and also... I have four live-in lovers that I'm pretty much married to."

"Polygamy?" my brother blurted.

"Ah... no, probably not in the way you're thinking of it. It's more polyamory, or polyandry." I'd spent some time researching the terms knowing this would probably come up.

"You're... married... to all three of them?" my father

said, his voice tight as if the shock was starting to strangle him.

"Four," I corrected. Aethan wasn't around at the mome—

A horse neighed off in the distance and came galloping along the beach toward us. Aethan. Well, that would need to be explained as well at some point. Might as well just rip all the bandages off and do it now.

"Where's the other one?" my sister asked, looking just a little too eagerly at Del and Keph, devouring them with her eyes as Aethan trotted up to us and shifted to his satyr form.

"Hello!" he said jovially.

Everyone gaped, mouth open, eyes wide, and I burst out laughing.

My sister glared at me and I tried to suck it back in, but if their expressions had gotten any bigger they would have looked like cartoon characters.

"You were a horse—" my brother gasped.

"H-his legs—" my father stammered.

"He's naked too—" my sister said, her cheeks turning bright red.

I sighed. "Aethan, I thought we talked about how I was going to make the introductions and explain everything before we showed them your other forms. Remember that conversation?"

He just grinned and snorted, sounding very much like the horse he'd just been.

"Other forms?" my father asked.

"Yeah, it's a lot to take in. Why don't you come inside where it's a bit cooler and I'll explain everything."

Once we were all up in the living area, I made the formal introductions. "This is Delphon, Kephas, Hyperion whom you've already met, and Aethan." To my guys, I said, "This is my father, David Chambers, my brother Daniel Chambers, and my sister Sheri Chambers."

They all stared at each other, the awkward silence stretching on and on and—

"Can I get anyone a drink?" I asked.

It was a long and arduous afternoon as I slowly explained everything to my family. My sister took it the best, I think. Though she kept not-so-subtly looking at the various swaying bits of my guys. My father was confused, then angry, then confused, then shocked, then just seemed dazed and worn out. My brother didn't seem to like any of this. Of course, I also had to explain about his wedding, since he recognized a couple of the guys from that disaster. So I didn't blame him for being upset, at least for now. I guess we'd see if he ever forgave me for that debacle.

As evening fell, I escorted my family back to the portal, while the guys trailed along a good few steps behind.

"What do we tell people?" my father asked. "If they ask where you are?"

"I've been saying I'm moving to the tropics and I'll be hard to get ahold of."

"Yes." He nodded. "That should work."

"How *do* we get ahold of you?" my brother's tone still held a bit of scorn. He was too straight-laced and high-strung to accept my new life situation so easily, or forget about the mess I'd made of his wedding.

"That will be hard. I'm working on something, but I haven't got it figured out yet. For now, I'll call you whenever I return to your world."

"Your world," my father said, still sounding dazed. "Other worlds." He just shook his head.

"Think of it like Narnia," my sister said, taking my dad's arm to help him along.

I took them back through the portal and made sure they were safe in taxis before I returned.

"I like your family," Keph said in his low rumble where he and the others had waited for me to return by the rocks. "We should visit them in your world sometime."

Yeah, that would be interesting.

"Sure," I said and continued on up to the house. That hadn't gone quite as well as it could have, but the guys consoled me that night and by the time I fell asleep, snuggled with all of them in my bed, I was quite relaxed and already forgetting the incident.

CHAPTER 28

THE NEXT DAY, JANICE PICKED ME UP FROM THE ALLEY AND drove me to a café nearby. We didn't speak much in the car on the way there, and it wasn't until we were settled at a table, coffees in hand, that she finally spoke.

"I'm sorry Annie," she said a bit sheepishly. "I..." She shook her head and because of our bond, I got the sense that she was still trying to apologize for killing Hera.

I reached over, taking one of her hands in mine.

"The more I think about it, the more I realize you were right, and had to make a very hard choice." I gave her a reassuring smile. "I couldn't have done it. I hated her, but I still couldn't have."

"I know," she said softly. "And I could." She pressed her lips tight for a long moment. "I was worried you'd hate me. You've been out of contact for so long, I..."

I squeezed her hand. "I just had a lot to do, and while I did it, well, you were always in the back of my mind. I didn't know how to say what I needed to say until now. And what I need to say is: thank you, Janice."

She sighed heavily, nodding, her gaze dropping to our joined hands. "Good. 'Cause I just kept thinking about it, running things over and over in my head, and I can't see any way she wouldn't have rained hell down upon us if she'd lived. She still had far too much power and wealth at her disposal, and we had no idea how long she'd survive with her immortality gone. I know I did the right thing, even if it wasn't the moral thing."

"Hey," I said, giving her fingers another squeeze and drawing her gaze back up to me. It was clear she'd tortured herself over this and it broke my heart that she'd think I hate her for it.

"Thank you," I said, willing her to *feel* through our bond how much I appreciated what she'd done for us.

She gave me a tight nod and a soft smile. Yes, it had been six weeks, but killing Hera wasn't something she was just going to be able to get over.

"Okay then," I said brightly, determined to change the subject to something happier. "I had another reason for wanting to speak to you."

"Oh?"

"Ah, yeah. I was hoping I could give my family your number to contact you if they needed to get ahold of me. They... I told them about the other world. Showed them actually."

Janice snorted. "How did that turn out? Did they meet your hot as hell, buck-naked harem?" she chortled.

"Yeah." I rolled my eyes at her. "And it went as well as could be expected."

"Oh, the price you have to pay to live with those guys

in paradise," she said, her sad smile turning into an all-out grin.

"Which is where you come in. Since you can open portals, I thought you'd be the best go between if my family needs to get ahold of me. I know that's a bit of an imposition, but—"

She waved at me, cutting me off. "Of course I will."

"Wonderful. Thank you again. And," I said, drawing out the word, "that will give you an excuse to come and visit."

"Ah, yeah," Janice quirked an odd smile. "I may visit more often than that, we'll see." I was about to ask what she meant when she said, "I left the FBI."

"Oh?" That was news. "Didn't you like it there?"

"I did, very much, but... I've changed just a little too much to go back to my old life."

"Because of me," I said softly.

"Yes," she said and it was her turn to squeeze my hand. "But not in a bad way. I'm still trying to accept some things about me. Like my wings, but overall, I feel a lot more... empowered now than I did before. I don't know what I want to do, but I feel like I can do anything I put my mind to." She shrugged. "I was thinking I might try my hand as a private detective. Not sure though."

"Janice... P.I...." I blinked. "You know, in all the time we've known each other, I don't think I've learned your last name."

"It's Leoni."

I tried again. "Janice Leoni, P.I. That has a certain ring to it."

She gave a bit of a laugh then sighed heavily. "Yeah,

we'll see if I go that route. I don't know what I'll do. I think I'll take a bit of time and figure that out. And while I do, I may want to visit the other world a bit more often and... find out more about... me."

"And see Naz?" I asked mischievously.

Her blush and grin told me everything I needed to know. "Maybe."

"We'd be happy to have you. We have one dedicated guest room and most nights there are other rooms available as well. You could stay with us—" She gave me an odd, slightly apprehensive look. "Or not."

"Ah... yeah, thank you for the offer, but if you're going to be bumping-uglies with those guys of yours, just remember little old me can *feel* it when you do. When I'm a world away, I'm fine, but staying in your house... might be a bit awkward."

Awkward to say the least. "Right, well, no worries. You can stay with Naz and bump-your-own-uglies."

Her blush deepened and swept down her neck. "Ah, yeah, no..." She rolled her eyes and laughed. "Well... maybe. We'll see."

I laughed with her. I wouldn't push her toward Naz, but I had a good feeling about him and Janice, and with everything that had happened to her, she deserved some good, other-world sex with a hot guy.

CHAPTER 29

A FEW DAYS AFTER ANNIE TALKED WITH JANICE, I DECIDED it was time for me to finish things with my father. I'd been avoiding the conversation because I knew it wouldn't go well. But I also knew if I put it off for too long, my father would send men to look for me, and I didn't want to face him from a weakened position.

No, better to confront him, show him my bonded mate, and be done with the monster once and for all.

Now we stood in front of my old house. The deck around the house was a large expanse of wood, which projected well out from the trees to give an amazing view of the Syltheorin River—where it cut through a lush and green valley—and the Ophion Mountains beyond. There were no railings on things in the *erinai* world, high in the trees of Phyllidian Forest, but I wasn't worried about Annie falling over the edge. She could float using Del's powers if she needed to.

"Gods, this view..." Annie said, her voice hushed and reverent.

I nodded. It was an amazing view, but everything to do with this house, this place, was tainted for me.

Annie looked at me then, perhaps because of my silence. She slid her hand into mine. "You are stronger than you know," she said softly. "I know this isn't easy for you."

It wasn't, but she was right. I had her... and the others —though they were back at our house at the moment. And I did feel stronger. The flight here had been quicker than any other time before.

Usually it took me the better part of two days to fly across the large island, resting occasionally and sleeping at night. I hadn't been certain how long it would take while carrying Annie, but she'd used Del's powers to make herself lighter, and through our bond, she'd shared some of Keph's strength and Aethan's speed and endurance. Because of that, I'd felt refreshed the entire way and made the trip in one long day of travel, and despite the sunset with its oranges, reds, and purples staining the sky and draping the forest in deep shadows, I knew we'd return home once I'd said my piece. I drew myself up and went to the door to the house in which I'd grown up and firmly knocked.

It was my mother who answered. Hades would turn cold before my father ever did anything as mundane as answer a door.

"Hyp?" My mother's eyes went wide and she strode out to embrace me. "It's so good to see you."

"Hyp?" Annie asked behind me.

I extricated myself from my mother's hug and stepped back. "Mother, this is Annie, my bonded." To Annie, I added, "I like my other short form better, but I couldn't convince my family to use it."

My mother stared at Annie, stunned for a second, then she smiled. But I knew that smile. It was the awkward smile which said, 'I don't like this, and I don't know what to say, so I'll smile a bit too brightly.'

Annie approached my mother and embraced her. My mother followed suit after a long awkward moment of standing there. It was clear she was surprised that I'd bonded to a non-*erinai,* but I'd known this would be her reaction and I'd warned Annie before we'd left.

"I've come to talk to Father," I said stoically. "And introduce Annie."

Oh, the feathers I was about to ruffle.

Mother's eyes went wide behind Annie's back. She shook her head ever so subtly. "Ah... Annie? Nice to meet you." My mother's words were a bit halting. "Your father is... unavailable."

I doubted that, and I wasn't coming back. I was getting this over and done with and then moving on.

I'd never lived up to my father's expectation and knew he wouldn't accept Annie. But I wanted to make it clear she was my bonded, she wasn't a lie I'd made up to get out of my responsibilities, and that I was never going to be the *erinai* he wanted me to be.

I strode past my mother into the large house and called out, "Father! It's Hyperion! We need to talk."

My mother gasped and I smiled. I'd never been so forthright with him because I'd been afraid of what he'd do. And now I didn't care.

Heavy footfalls sounded on the floor above me letting

me know my father was indeed around, and he strode down the stairs with all the pomp and arrogance I'd come to know from him. His pristine white hair fell in perfect waves down to precisely an inch above his shoulders. Even at his age, he was fit and well-muscled, as tall as I, but larger through chest and shoulders. A consummate warrior.

His pale blue eyes were hard as he stared me down, and for the first time in my life I matched that stare without fear. I even smiled, knowing it would infuriate him.

"Father," I said with the exact amount of respect someone of his station deserved and not a bit more.

"Hyperion," he growled. "You've been gone too long. You have duties here you've ignored. There will be a reckoning for that." His lips grew tight, his jaw tense. "I thought I'd taught you more respect."

"I don't care what you think I should be doing. I never accepted the position of Sky General, you just assumed I would. And I haven't come back to take it either. I've come back to introduce you to my bonded."

His brows furrowed. "You've been nowhere near the forest. Where did you meet an *erinai* woman?"

I couldn't help but smile even larger. "Oh, I didn't. She's not even from this world. This is Annie." I half stepped back and waved to introduce her.

She strode forward radiating all the stunning, confident power that I knew she possessed.

My father's eyes widened. "What... is she?" he hissed.

"Beautiful, strong, loving, intelligent, passionate,

independent, caring. She's defeated a goddess. Can you say as much, Father?"

He was sputtering, his mouth opening and closing, so angry he couldn't form a coherent sentence. "She's not one of us!"

"Oh, dear," I heard my mother say, now hiding a little behind the open door. She knew how angry my father could get.

"Hello, General Eonas," Annie said, keeping with the same respect I'd shown him, and she dipped her head in a slight bow. "It's not at all a pleasure to meet you. I can see now why you left home, Rion."

"How dare you come into my home and—" My father stalked toward her with an arm raised to slap her. With Aethan's speed and Keph's strength Annie landed a solid blow to the man's jaw before he could hit her and he went down in a heap.

He sat there, blinking for a long moment.

"Don't you ever presume to lay a hand on me, sir," she said softly. As he rose, she continued. "Now, I think Rion has some words for you as well."

She turned her back on him and made for the door, but stopped in the open entranceway and turned back.

"Oh, and you should know, Rion has already impregnated me. We're going to have a litter of half-breed babies. But don't worry, we won't name any of them after you." She smiled beatifically, then left.

I knelt next to my still recovering father, not waiting for him to stand and regain his composure.

"She's something, isn't she?" I chuckled. "Now, here's the plan. I'm going to leave and probably never return.

There's nothing for me here. You drove my sister to her death, sapped the spirit from Mother, and the only friends I had were ones mandated by you in the military. I have new friends now. A new family. We have a home on the beach near Masia. Perhaps someday, you can come and visit and see all your grandchildren, but I suggest you get your attitude straight before you do. Step one foot inside my house in belligerence, hatred, and anger, and you'll face so much more than that little tap Annie gave. Do you understand me?"

My father glared at me. "Get out!"

He spat at me, blood leaking from the split lip Annie had given him. She hadn't held back. Good.

"Happy to." I stood and strode to the door. There, I spoke loud enough that my father could hear. "I have a loving home, in which you'd be welcome, if you like, Mother. You don't ever have to see him or face his rage again."

She stared at me, her eyes wide with shock and fear.

"I won't be back," I added, "but know that my door will always be open for you."

"How dare you!" my father roared from inside. "Get out!"

I waited for my mother's response, hoping, praying, she'd say something.

We stared at each other. I didn't think she was aware that I was waiting for her response, she was so used to father speaking for her.

Finally, she blinked, realization flashing through her expression. "Oh... Hyp, I..." She glanced inside at the hulking form of the man I no longer considered to be my father. "I... can't leave him."

And there it was. I didn't know why she chose to stay, but it was her choice.

I nodded, then gave her a kiss on the cheek. "Goodbye, Mother."

I turned away from her, a part of me hoping that someday she'd find her way to Masia. I wanted to be there for her, but I couldn't stay. I wouldn't have that monster involved in my new life with Annie in any way.

Annie waited for me at the edge of the long balcony, and I picked her up, and flew away.

"How did that feel?" she asked once we were well away.

"Horrible," I said, the weight that I was sure would always be there, heavy in my chest. "But it was necessary." And as I said the words, the weight shifted to sadness, edged with relief.

I'd done what I'd never had the courage to do, freed myself to live my life, not the life that had always been expected of me.

Annie nodded, holding me close. "It felt good to clock your father," she murmured against my neck. "Sorry if I stole some of your thunder doing that."

I shook my head. "I don't think he's ever had anyone stand up to him, let alone a woman. It was... the most perfect thing I've ever seen."

She giggled. "Good."

"One thing," I asked, leaning back to look her in the eyes, more than a little curious. "Was that true what you said about being pregnant?"

Her face lit up with a brilliant smile. "Yep. I'm fairly certain I am. It can't surprise you, given how much I've been with all of you guys. Though I have no clue whose child it is. I guess we'll see when he or she comes."

A stunning swell of pride and joy swept through me. I hadn't realized how much I wanted to be a father until that moment and while I hoped the child was mine, I realized I didn't care. Even if he or she didn't have wings, they'd still be my child. All of ours. Another member to our amazing family.

I smiled and hugged Annie a little closer, surging higher into the sky, speeding home. I was sure the others would want to hear this amazing news as well.

CHAPTER 30

AETHAN

Rion had returned with Annie looking happier than I'd ever seen him, and while I knew he was thrilled with Annie's news about having a baby, I also knew it was because he'd closed the book on his relationship with his father.

Something I felt I needed to do. I didn't have a terrible relationship with my family, but that was because I didn't really have one with them. And while I didn't have someone I needed to confront, a part of me wanted to show Annie where I came from and why I didn't belong.

So, a few days later, I invited Annie to join me, shifted into my horse form, and we took off.

It felt good to let loose and gallop, and it was even better with Annie riding bareback on me. I didn't fully understand it—something about the power she shared with Janice—but she was a far better rider now, easily moving and staying in place while I ran full-out in my horse form.

She let out whoops and calls every now and then,

sounding so free and excited, and it made me run just a little bit faster, just to see if I could make her call out again.

But there was a point to this ride. I was taking Annie to see my home, such as it was, and soon she'd see why I'd wanted to leave. Something I knew I had to share with her, but didn't really want to.

I took comfort in knowing that I'd found my herd, that I was no longer a misfit among the people who were supposed to love me, but this was still a journey I hadn't wanted to make.

And then I crested a hill and we were there. The great plains where I used to live.

Off in the distance stood a massive shifting heard of horses, meandering slowly over the plains, and moving among them were perhaps a dozen satyrs.

"These are my people," I said. It was always just a little awkward speaking in horse form, too much lip and teeth.

"There are so few of them," Annie said softly.

I swung my large head around to look at her. "It's not just the satyrs. All those horses are my people, too."

Her eyes widened. "Oh."

"Now you see," I said, shaking my head. "They prefer this form. Easier to graze. They don't want to worry about the world of men. They wish only to live wild on the plains."

"Oh."

"Exactly. I don't mind my horse form. It's a part of who I am, but only a part. It gets me places quickly, but I don't want to be an animal all the time. I want to be a man. I want to hold myself to a higher standard of intelligence and awareness."

Annie dismounted, easily hopping off and landing lightly, and I shifted back to my satyr form.

Together we watched the slow, shifting herd out on the plains for a long moment, letting the warm breeze sweep over us and the clouds lazily drift by.

"They never really understood me," I said softly. Annie's hand slipped into mine, giving it a squeeze. "Oh, don't get me wrong, I don't really understand them either. I was happy to get away and I don't think they really missed me."

"It's still sad," she said softly. "They're your family."

I looked at her. "No, Annie. You and Rion and Del and Keph are my family."

She kissed me softly on the lips, an action I was still getting used to after all this time. When she stepped back her hand rose to stroke her stomach.

I smiled. A child was on the way, though still some time off, and it made me happy beyond reason.

"Soon, our family will be a bit larger," she said with a soft smile. She looked up at me. "Thank you for bringing me here. I don't think I fully understood, until now."

I nodded. "The people here are in many ways stuck in the past. I want to move into the future."

She nodded. "Do you want to talk to anyone?"

"No." There wasn't anyone who'd understand. They never had.

"Then let's go home," she said.

I shifted back to a horse and she was quickly on my back.

With a whoop and holler from Annie, I was off, galloping once again.

I was glad I'd shown her where I'd come from, glad I'd said goodbye to the part of me that had been a part of my people, but I wouldn't trade anything for the family I shared now. It was everything I ever wanted, and I couldn't wait to see what our future held.

CHAPTER 31

KEPH

THE EVENING AETHAN AND ANNIE RETURNED FROM THE Theophylian Plains, Annie took me for a walk on the beach and asked if I wanted to introduce her to my family, since my family was the only one she had yet to meet.

"Are you certain you don't want to go?" Annie asked me.

I nodded. "It's a long trip back to see my family and I have no quick way to get there, like the others. By the time we got there and back, you'd probably be due." I replied. "We can wait until after the child is born. Though I fear it would be a bit of a let-down for all involved."

"Why would you say that?"

I sighed and turned my gaze to the sunset, the beautiful end to another warm, calm day. "You have to understand, my people are a lot like stone itself. We're hard and unfeeling about a lot of things. They're set in their ways and don't change easily. That's not to say they wouldn't welcome you, but their welcome would be... cold. Not because they don't like you, but because everything they do is cold. It's just who they are, distant and..." I gave a bit of a laugh. "Stony."

"Oh," she said softly.

"I'm sure my father and mother would love to meet you, but their love and reception would seem like a hard, cold indifference to you."

"Really?"

I nodded. "And you to them would be so vastly different from anything they know. You're so warm and welcoming, and... soft." As I said this, I reached over to trace a finger down her shoulder and arm, then slipped my hand around her waist and hugged her gently against my side. "They wouldn't understand you. They'd try to love you for my sake, but you'd be so foreign to them. I can see it now. When we leave, they'd just shake their heads and shrug, and go back to their lives."

"It sounds like a lonely and distant life." Annie leaned into me a little as we walked, snuggling close in my embrace.

"It was. That was one of the reasons I wanted to leave. I could have been at home there, but I'd always expressed my feelings a little more than the others, which made me odd. I was curious, another odd trait. So, they let me go and explore the world. I found so many wonders. I couldn't understand why they wanted to stay buried deep in their mountains. I love my family, but this new family with you and the others is so much warmer and more welcoming."

We were silent for a long time until Annie asked, "If

this child is yours, what would your family think of that, a half-stone-titan?"

I chuckled. "They wouldn't be upset or curious. They would accept it with the same stoic coldness they accept everything. No shock or horror, like I suspect Rion's father would have if the child was his, just a nod and then back to their lives. They'd love it, but... not in a way you'd feel from them."

Annie shivered next to me. "So cold."

"Exactly."

"I'm glad you're so warm," she said, kissing my biceps.

That, more than anything she'd ever said, struck my heart.

"Thank you." But still... "I sometimes wish I was softer and not as big. I feel awkward at times and... well I know I can't really hurt you since you have my own powers of durability, but..." I didn't really have the words. "I just want to be a bit more like the rest of you some days."

"Oh, Keph, no! You should be proud and happy to be you. I like your... hardness," she said that with a hitch and a silly grin. I felt her shiver with satisfaction and snuggle even closer. "You're wonderful as you are."

"But I'll never be able to visit Del's home, or Rion's, I'm too big, too heavy, too awkward."

"From what I saw of Rion's home, you're not missing much. As for Del's you could get there eventually by just walking. But that doesn't matter. You're wonderful just as you are. You are a part of our family now and we accept you with love and openness and wonder."

I smiled and drew in a deep breath, letting that sink

in for a long moment. She was right. I was welcome and accepted with them, not just with the cold acceptance of all things like my family, but with a warmth and joy that I'd never known elsewhere. I could be proud to be me.

"Thank you," I murmured.

Annie tried to reach an arm around me, but only just managed to get to the other side of my broad back. She gave it a vigorous rub and pressed closer.

"We all have each other," she said a bit dreamily. "That's all that matters."

And with those words, for the first time, in my entire life, I finally felt like I had a home.

CHAPTER 32

DELPHON

AFTER RION AND AETHAN HAD DEALT WITH THEIR families, I knew I'd be happier dealing with mine. Except I didn't want to say a far-off goodbye like Aethan had, or have a confrontation like Rion... even though I knew a confrontation was inevitable. I didn't want to lose my relationship with my sister, brother, or father, and I was afraid my mother would force the issue, which was why I'd been avoiding the trip home.

Annie had also insisted on coming with me, and that she was going to do it without a huphelopoid. So, it was even easier to put it off until after she'd given birth to little Petra—a not-as-tiny-as-Annie-would-have-liked stone titan girl.

Then Annie announced that she needed to drown herself, saying the powers she'd gotten from Janice meant she would adapt and be able to breathe water.

Which had been a horrible idea!

But she'd insisted, and I'd been there to pull her out —after she'd nearly died, of course!

We'd resuscitated her in a panic, the other guys just as frustrated with her as I was, and she'd rested for a day and tried again, and sure enough, after almost drowning, she could now breathe water.

Except I was pretty sure I'd aged at least a decade from the experience.

We left Petra in the care of Keph, Rion, and Aethan, along with a wet nurse from the town, and Annie escorted me back to Galniosia.

She'd become an amazing swimmer in the short time that we'd lived in our seaside home. She still couldn't compete when I had my tail, but without it, she was nearly a match for me, lithe and graceful and the most beautiful thing I'd ever seen in the water.

And, even though I didn't have my powers over water in this world, she still did, and could use that to jet through the water even faster than I swam with my triton's tail.

It was amazing to watch her move with such ease, but, as we drew close to my old home, my mind turned from my attractive companion to the 'battle' ahead.

I'd been going out nearly every day over the past nine months, sometimes for most of the day, searching for pearls, and I'd managed to collect a little more than a half a dozen so far. I'd hoped for more, but I knew they were rare, hence why they were so valuable.

Seven tritons had died during the two attacks on Hera, which meant I owed my mother and Galniosia three hundred and fifty pearls, and I had a long way still to go. At my current rate, it would take me well over fifty years to repay the kingdom.

But I was bringing another gift which I hoped would diminish my debt, the item secured in a long box made of treated wood, which resisted water. This was the one trophy I'd taken from Hera's estate. It was a bit awkward to swim with the box, but we'd still made good time.

Poseia met us outside of the Hall of Light and her eyes widened at the sight of Annie without a huphelopoid.

"How...?" she asked.

"Long story," Annie said. "The short version is I can breathe water now."

Poseia huffed a half laugh, deciding to just go with it, then turned to me, her expression darkening. "Mother is in a foul mood today. Be careful."

"If I was careful, sister, I'd never have gotten myself where I am today, as good and bad as that is."

She nodded to that. "If you can't be careful, be wise."

"Good luck with that," Annie said softly.

That made Poseia chuckle. "Fine, if you can't be careful or wise, be..." She searched for a word. "Daring."

"That," I said, squaring my shoulders, "I can do."

We entered the Hall of Light with its spectacular ribbons of light coming from the surface, and even from a distance I could see the displeasure on my mother's face, and the exhaustion on my father's. This was going to be a challenge indeed.

Luarnon floated a bit farther to one side than usual as if trying to stay out of my mother's line-of-sight and therefore her line-of-fire. There was a young triton woman with him, and I took this to be the bride I'd avoided and he'd acquired. I didn't know if they'd been married yet or not, but they seemed happy, staying close to each other, whispering and keeping to themselves.

"What do you want, Exiled One?" my mother bellowed down the hall before we'd even made it halfway to her throne.

"That's what she's taken to calling you," Poseia whispered, still escorting us.

"Be quick and be gone. I don't wish you in my sight for any longer than necessary."

"I really want to slap her one," Annie hissed, low enough that only I and Poseia could hear.

"Let's not," I said. Then we were close enough that I stopped and bowed. "Dearest Queen and King of Galniosia. I bring to you part of what is owed."

My mother raised a brow at that.

Even Poseia, still in the water not far away, turned back to me. She mouthed the word, 'already?' and I drew forth a pouch.

From it, I withdrew the seven pearls I'd found so far. "This is only a small sum of my payment," I said, giving the pearls over to Poseia who took them to our mother.

"Seven?" Mother said with distain. "You owe us fifty times as much!"

I did indeed.

"That's not all I brought," I said and sank to the floor of the hall, my tail brushing its smooth tiles, to set down the long box and undo the clasps holding it closed.

My mother remained silent, which hopefully meant she was curious. Even my father perked up a little.

I made sure, when I opened the box, it was facing away from the thrones so they couldn't see the trident which lay within, and when I pulled it out, I held it up saying, "Behold the trident of Poseidon!"

Poseia and Luarnon gasped and my father's eyes went wide.

My mother to her credit, showed only the barest moment of shock, then was stony-faced once again.

It was a magnificent weapon, made from a strange green-blue metal. Tracings on the three sharp prongs and down the long haft were intricate, depicting all manner of sea-life, and inlaid in the handle, were a few aquamarine gems, and pearls, dozens of them.

I swam slowly toward the thrones, the haft across my open hands, unthreatening, and presented it to them.

I knew it was Poseidon's own trident as it had been labelled as such in Hera's treasure room.

"We found this when we defeated Hera. Something she'd claimed from the God of the Sea long ago. I give it to you, the rightful rulers of the sea." Well... only of this part of the sea, but I wasn't going to quibble.

My mother rose slowly and reached out to lift the trident from my hands and inspect it.

"It's magnificent!" she whispered. "The detail and the material, so light, yet strong." She gave it a few test strikes, then looked at me. The awe on her face was slowly replaced with disdain once again. "This will go a long way toward repaying your debt," she said, voice proclamatory.

"Oh Hades, Hanea! You're still going to ask for more?" My father had risen from his throne. "This gift is priceless! Surely it repays his debt."

She shot him a long, hot look, her jaw tight. "Do you so easily dismiss the lives he so casually threw away?"

"Of course not. And if you're going to proclaim he was so casual then state their names, each of the fallen seven, right now," the king countered.

I tried not to smile at his bravado.

My mother's expression turned sour. She didn't know their names. "Still their lives—"

"Are irreplaceable, yes. They are priceless, yes?" the king said.

"Yes!"

"As is the gift you're holding. One priceless gift for another should suffice," he huffed.

"I won't let him off that easily." She turned back to me.

It was at that point that a quick current of water brushed past me and Annie was suddenly in front of my mother, barely inches apart. Her hair floated behind her like a pale red cape and she was well flushed with emotion.

"I have stood by and listened to this for long enough!"

"You!" my mother countered. Then she blinked. "How are you... You're not..." It seemed she'd only then begun to pay any attention to Annie and realized she didn't have a huphelopoid.

"You want to know how I swim as I do? How I breathe water? It's simple. I'm the one who defeated Hera. I have powers over water and can adapt to any environment. I'm not a goddess. I don't seek to be worshiped. But I have killed a goddess and let me tell you, you are nothing compared to her."

My mother's eyes widened and she shied away, her back bumping the back of her throne.

Annie backed off then, composing herself and drawing herself up.

"Tell me," she said softly. "What is it you hold against Delphon? Why do you despise him so much? He's your son."

The fire returned to my mother's eyes. "Exactly. I knew my duty! I gave everything for this kingdom, and yet he always shirked his responsibility. He didn't take anything seriously. He's a lazy, simpering, worthless child."

"Is he?" Annie asked, her expression eerily serene. "That's not the man I've known at all. He's loyal and responsible. He's strong and dedicated. He risked his life to save two worlds, not just your small kingdom. And those seven tritons you throw in his face, they did the same. They gave their lives for this world and another. I think that deserves a little respect. And I think this gift shows Delphon's respect for you and for the sacrifice those seven tritons made."

My mother sneered at her. "I can see you're a strong woman, such as myself. Don't worry, he'll disappoint you, fail you, betray you."

"He never has and never will," Annie replied with certainty, making my heart swell at her love.

"Does he do everything you tell him to do?" my mother shot back.

Annie took a long pause before answering. She looked back at me, smiling, then at the others in the room before turning back to my mother. "I don't tell him to do anything. I make no commands. I ask and he is more than willing to help, because... he loves me."

Oh Hades! She just told my mother that I didn't love her.

My mother's eyes went wide.

Poseia nearly choked.

My mother sputtered for a moment and Annie kept going. "If you had shown him the love of a mother instead of the harsh hand of a queen, perhaps he'd have been different. But then... you'd never have driven him away, and I'd never have met him. So I guess I do have something to thank you for. Did I mention we were bonded, mother-in-law?"

My father's eyes went wide. He looked to me for confirmation and I nodded with a grin.

Annie pushed on, her voice even and calm, revealing just how powerful she really was with her relaxed confidence. "I do hope, that in the years to come, you'll come to see him differently, as I have. I hope you'll come to our home, on the beach near Masia. I hope you'll want to visit your grandchildren. We haven't had any half-tritons yet, but I'm certain we will. And when that day comes, if you wish to reconcile and make peace with your son, I'm certain he'll forgive you."

I approached with an air of penitence. I didn't want this battle to continue and I didn't want the rest of my family to have to pick sides. "There's no need to wait for that day. I know you were only doing the best you could, and I know I wasn't the son you wished you'd had. But I've come to learn what it means to love and be loved, what it means to serve instead of being served. I understand your sacrifice, Mother. I forgive you."

My mother blinked, looking back and forth between me and Annie. Her gaze settled on me and it wasn't entirely displeased. "You've... changed."

Annie must have been shifting the eddies around herself with my water magic as she didn't otherwise move, yet she drifted back, away from the queen, to give me more room.

"I have," I said, bowing my head in respect.

When I looked up again, my mother's stern look had returned and she drew herself up. She looked at the trident and said, "This is a most precious gift and it shall repay the most precious sacrifice of our people." Well that was a start. "And..." this in a softer tone I'd so rarely heard from her. "I should like to see my grandchildren, when I have some." She looked back and forth from me to Annie again. "Even if they are with a fiery, god-killing, human woman." She sighed then. "One whose heart is true and who loves my son. That much I can see plainly."

Annie smiled. "Thank you, your majesty."

"Good!" Suddenly my mother was all business once more. "And thank you for this precious gift. Will you be returning to the shore immediately?"

That was a surprise question, implying that we didn't have to make a hasty retreat as I'd expected. "Would you like us to stay?" I wouldn't mind spending a bit of time with my family, if the option was on the table. I turned to Annie. "Would you like to stay?"

She nodded, giving me a warm smile. "Of course."

My mother gave a tight nod. "I think I'd like to get to

know this new daughter of mine. She's... full of fire... like me." My mother returned to her throne and sat, the trident across her lap. "Please stay for a bit." And then she actually smiled.

A small, intimate dinner was prepared—my mother was willing to meet Annie, but not publicly announce her to our people—and during the meal I learned Luarnon would be returning with his newly bonded to the Atargatine Merfolk kingdom and Poseia had taken the mantle of heir and would succeed my parents when they died or stepped down.

I congratulated them both as Annie chatted up the foreign princess, giggling together for half the meal, and for the first time in a long time, I felt comfortable in the palace.

Something that never would have happened if I hadn't met Annie.

CHAPTER 33

ANNIE

A LITTLE LESS THAN A YEAR LATER, I LEARNED THAT THE adaptation power I'd acquired from Janice included the rigors of childbirth. Petra had been more than ten hours of sweaty, screaming, painful—very, very painful—labor. She hadn't been a small baby. She was half stone titan after all, but when little Cupid was born—our half-*erinai* bundle of joy—it was a breeze.

There'd only been enough pain to let me know things were happening and when to push, and only for barely an hour's worth of time. The tiny child had the cutest little wings, which were completely ineffective, thank the gods, since I couldn't imagine what a flying newborn child would be like, and I recovered quickly.

A week later we invited all our friends for a party in celebration of the new baby.

Janice came and brought Naz as her plus one. She'd been visiting him frequently, often stopping in at our house because we were so close to the portal. Poseia, Del's sister, had come as had a few people from Masia with whom we'd become close, one of whom had been the some-times wet nurse for Petra, a *nereia* woman named Zona. She'd had a child around the time I'd had Petra, and had just had another, so there was a good chance we'd be keeping her on as a wet-nurse for Cupid when I wasn't available.

My father and sister had come. Daniel, my brother, still wasn't over my odd relationship with my guys, nor me ruining his wedding. He'd sent a card, though, which I hoped was a first step in reconciliation.

The others had brought gifts as well. The guys had made Cupid a crib. Well, they'd made a *new* crib, since we already had one for Petra. And since they'd learned from the making of the last one, this one was sturdier, so we'd moved Petra into it—her being a much heavier and larger child.

My father had bought the new baby a bunch of onesies—that were adorable!—only to then notice how no one was really wearing much of anything. He said he'd return them and get something else, and I told him the bonus to that was that we'd get to see him again, sooner than usual.

Zona made a beautiful sling-wrap in which I could carry Cupid. She was wearing one herself with her new baby asleep inside, and my sister had brought a variety of small tropical plants. Less a gift for the child as it was something to spruce up the area around our house.

She also showed off her diamond ring and my guys made the appropriate noises—once I'd told them what the ring had meant. She was engaged to a baker who had a shop down from hers in the same plaza.

But Janice had brought possibly the best gift of all: chocolate. It wasn't something I could get in this world and I knew I'd truly treasure and savor every last bite. Poseia brought several beautiful shell-based pieces of jewelry, that the queen had insisted she give us. She said she knew I probably wouldn't wear them, but we could use them to barter in the town for supplies as our family grew, which made me laugh, because it was Poseia being practical as ever.

Now we all sat in the covered living area, drinking fruit juices and chatting, while little Petra toddled around on the porch moving from person to person loving all the attention. She'd grown a lot, not even twelve months old yet, and was now over three feet tall. She was going to be big like her father. If it hadn't been for the strength I'd acquired being bonded to Keph, I probably wouldn't have been able to pick her up anymore. She was heavy and ate... a lot. I'd been horrified the first time I'd found her eating dirt and pebbles.

Keph had been watching her playing outside, and I'd come to join them and nearly fainted. But Keph assured me that such things were actually a part of a growing stone titan's diet. He then proceeded to pop a small stone in his mouth and chew on it, quite happily. Apparently, there were some things about this world I still hadn't gotten used to.

As evening set in, my father and sister left, but everyone else stayed. Poseia was going to stay the night as it was a bit of a trip back to Galniosia, and she chatted with the others, while Janice and I went for a walk.

Even though she still lived in the other world and we

didn't talk often, we still shared a bond and I felt closer to her than anyone else other than my guys.

"So," I asked. "How are things?"

"Not bad. My P.I. caseload is slowly building, and I'm actually starting to get clients referred by previous clients, so that's a good thing."

"That's great!" I said.

"Yeah. This new role is certainly interesting." Janice had built up a business as a private investigator for the last sixteen months or so, and the job had morphed into a semi-permanent gig with the Chicago police as a consulting investigator. She was often hired by others to look into things the police didn't have time for, cases of lower importance. When she solved them, she'd hand the case over to the police all nicely wrapped up and they'd take it from there. She got a bit of a stipend from the police and often a bit from those who hired her, and it added up to enough to live off of.

"But I feel like it's still doing what I did at the FBI, just for less money," she said. "It's good work and I like helping these people who otherwise wouldn't be helped, but it's still not... quite right."

"Maybe that's because you're not quite where you're supposed to be yet," I said.

She glanced at me. She must have sensed what I was thinking because her cheeks turned pink before I could even ask.

"Like with Naz?" I teased. "How are things with him?"

Her blush deepened. "Good. He's joined up with one of the minotaurs and Rhou, the *panai*, and they've formed their own little mercenary company. He's been away a lot on jobs."

"And when he gets back, I'm sure he's excited to see you?" I knew this much because he'd occasionally come to me, asking to send messages to Janice.

"Unhun," she replied noncommittally.

Gods, but she was tight lipped.

"And?"

"And?" She turned to me, an innocent look in her eyes.

"How's it going. Have you two…?"

She groaned. "It's going well enough. I'm not like you Annie. I'm not a… passionate woman. I was a tomboy most of my life. I like guys, in that I prefer them to women, but I've never been really close to anyone. I was dedicated to my schooling, then my job. I didn't have time for guys in my life. Now that I do, I… I don't really know what to do with him."

Oh, there was so very much she could do with him! But I could see her discomfort and unease, which made me wonder…

"Are you…?" How to word this and not be insensitive. "Have you been… intimate with anyone before?"

"No," she said, the word tight and clipped.

"Ah." I sighed. "Then I'm sorry if I seemed to have been pushing you. I just thought… he's handsome and interested. I don't know him that well, but he doesn't seem like a jerk."

"No, he isn't. He's kind and sensitive, but also strong and well… yeah… you've seen him."

"I have." I reached over and rubbed her back. "Don't

be afraid to let things happen. And don't be afraid to make things happen if that's what you want. I guess, don't be afraid to wait, either." I wouldn't. I hadn't. But I wasn't her.

She nodded. "Thanks. Honestly, I can't imagine what life must be like for you, with four big, handsome guys. It must be exhausting! And now you're pretty much constantly pregnant. Isn't that rough?"

I laughed. "Not really. The first pregnancy was rough, yes, but with our powers, we adapt well. Cupid was a breeze. And I don't mind having four hunky guys constantly wanting to make me happy in every possible way. It's a dream."

"Yeah, I guess, when you put it that way."

"If you ever need any advice on anything, I'm just a portal away."

She huffed a laugh. "I might. Naz has been exceptionally patient with me, but he's suggested a couple things—sexual things—we could try that are... not kinky things, but... beginners' stuff and..." Gods, she was so awkward and stilted talking about anything to do with sex. Poor girl.

"I get the idea, yeah. I'm here if you need me." I meant it. I felt for the woman, only now experimenting and growing in her sexuality. She wasn't old, but she wasn't young either, mid-twenties or so, and I'd been experimenting since my late teens.

She nodded, blushing furiously.

We returned to the others. Naz gave Janice a chaste kiss on the cheek, which she returned in kind. It was growing late, though, so we all retired. Poseia slept in

Del's usual room. Janice said goodbye to Naz and returned through the portal, and he flew off soon after.

Zona said she'd stay the night and take care of Petra and Cupid, which meant I had a night alone with my guys. Before they'd come along, I'd always prized my space in bed, but now, I was a consummate snuggler.

We all curled up together, Keph behind Rion on one side, Aethan on the other, and Del tucked up behind Aethan, his feet tangled with mine. It was warm and intimate, but relaxed and peaceful. I reached out to each of them, stroking a shoulder or hip, arm or leg with a few words of love before we all closed our eyes and slept.

I had everything I'd ever dreamed of: a tropical house on a beach, and not one, but *four* men who loved me, and a meaningful life as a healer.

I slept well that night.

And every night thereafter.

Thank you so much for reading the Grecian Goddess Trilogy!

OTHER BOOKS BY TESSA COLE

THE NEPHILIM'S DESTINY SERIES

Destined Shadows, prequel story

Destined Darkness, book 1

Destined Blood, book 2

Destined Fire, book 3

Destined Storm, book 4

Destined Radiance, book 5

THE ANGEL'S FATE SERIES

Fated Bonds, book 1

Fated Winter, book 2

Fated Fear, book 3

Fated Despair, book 4

Fated Resolve, book 5

Fated Heart, book 6

THE GRECIAN GODDESS TRILOGY

Kiss of the Goddess, book 1

Power of the Goddess, book 2

Bonds of the Goddess, book 3

Printed in Great Britain
by Amazon